Julia cried out as the blunt truth slammed against her chest. Ryder gripped her hands.

"I'm sorry. It's my fault."

She squeezed his hands. "Stop. It's not your fault. I attracted this stalker somehow. I let him into our lives."

Ryder straightened his shoulders and gave her a little shake. "Let's put the blame where it belongs—on this maniac who's been terrorizing you and has now snatched your daughter. And let's deal with him."

"How? We don't know where he is. Or who he is."

"He'll find you, Julia."

"He wants me."

A chill zinged up her spine, and she hunched her shoulders. Ryder pulled her into his arms, which represented her only safe harbor these days. He wove his fingers through her hair, pulling her head back to look into her face.

"We'll get her back, and then I'll keep both of you safe forever...or die trying."

CAROL ERICSON

CIRCUMSTANTIAL MEMORIES

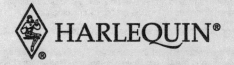

HARLEQUIN®

TORONTO • NEW YORK • LONDON
AMSTERDAM • PARIS • SYDNEY • HAMBURG
STOCKHOLM • ATHENS • TOKYO • MILAN • MADRID
PRAGUE • WARSAW • BUDAPEST • AUCKLAND

If you purchased this book without a cover you should be aware that this book is stolen property. It was reported as "unsold and destroyed" to the publisher, and neither the author nor the publisher has received any payment for this "stripped book."

To Neil, for these small hours,
these little wonders

Recycling programs
for this product may
not exist in your area.

ISBN-13: 978-0-373-69384-9
ISBN-10: 0-373-69384-2

CIRCUMSTANTIAL MEMORIES

Copyright © 2009 by Carol Ericson

All rights reserved. Except for use in any review, the reproduction or utilization of this work in whole or in part in any form by any electronic, mechanical or other means, now known or hereafter invented, including xerography, photocopying and recording, or in any information storage or retrieval system, is forbidden without the written permission of the publisher, Harlequin Enterprises Limited, 225 Duncan Mill Road, Don Mills, Ontario, Canada M3B 3K9.

This is a work of fiction. Names, characters, places and incidents are either the product of the author's imagination or are used fictitiously, and any resemblance to actual persons, living or dead, business establishments, events or locales is entirely coincidental.

This edition published by arrangement with Harlequin Books S.A.

® and TM are trademarks of the publisher. Trademarks indicated with ® are registered in the United States Patent and Trademark Office, the Canadian Trade Marks Office and in other countries.

www.eHarlequin.com

Printed in U.S.A.

ABOUT THE AUTHOR

Carol Ericson lives with her husband and two sons in Southern California, home of state-of-the-art cosmetic surgery, wild freeway chases, palm trees bending in the Santa Ana winds and a million amazing stories. These stories, along with hordes of virile men and feisty women clamor for release from Carol's head. It makes for some interesting headaches until she sets them free to fulfill their destinies and her readers' fantasies. To find out more about Carol, her books and her strange headaches, please visit her Web site at www.carolericson.com, "where romance flirts with danger."

Books by Carol Ericson

HARLEQUIN INTRIGUE

Don't miss any of our special offers. Write to us at the following address for information on our newest releases.

Harlequin Reader Service
U.S.: 3010 Walden Ave., P.O. Box 1325, Buffalo, NY 14269
Canadian: P.O. Box 609, Fort Erie, Ont. L2A 5X3

CAST OF CHARACTERS

Julia Rousseau—For four years, she's had no memory of a past that gave her a four-year-old daughter, but when Ryder McClintock materializes, memories of danger—and desire—flood her senses.

Ryder McClintock—When he returns to Colorado on leave from his latest covert ops assignment, he's stunned to discover the woman he loves...with no memory of their past together. Now he must reclaim her love, and his daughter, before a menace from Julia's past destroys their future.

Jeremy Scott—Julia's ex-husband and Ryder's ex-coworker died in a fiery explosion four years ago, but his evil continues to overshadow their lives.

Dr. Jim Brody—Julia's therapist seems to have more interest in getting close to Julia than helping her recover her memories.

Deputy Sheriff Zack Ballard—Do his suspicious actions link him to the threats against Julia, or does he have another secret?

Charlie Malone—This shy, bumbling mama's boy has a crush on Julia and resents the new man in her life.

Rosie Fletcher—A dead-ringer for Julia, she holds an important key to Julia's safety, but her amorous adventures put her life in danger.

Shelby Rousseau—Julia's daughter is the one person who kept Julia grounded during the dark days of her amnesia. But as the terror that engulfs Julia spreads to her daughter, will it bring Julia and Ryder closer together or tear them apart?

Chapter One

Julia glanced in her rearview mirror at the car gaining on her and muttered, *"Zut alors."* She clapped a hand over her mouth. She didn't know she could speak French.

She tried out a few more phrases, clean ones this time, and the words tumbled from her lips in an accent worthy of Pepé Le Pew. Shelby would be thrilled her mom could talk like one of her favorite cartoon characters.

And Dr. Brody, Jim, would be thrilled with this latest discovery—another key to her past.

The glare from the insistent headlights illuminated her car again as she pulled out of the curve. Why did this guy have his brights on? She accelerated on the straightaway, gripping the wheel with clammy hands.

This highway through the mountains always gave her the jitters, ever since she plowed over the guardrail almost four years ago in a howling blizzard.

Her neighbors, the Stokers, cautioned her against taking night classes at the university to prevent her from driving this road after dark, but she had to move beyond her fears. Besides she needed this class to finish her general education requirements and start taking her upper-division psychology courses. She'd just taken her final exam and opted out of the summer session, so she wouldn't have to make this drive at night until the fall.

The car behind her honked and she jumped, jerking the steering wheel to the right. *Go around me, you moron.* She didn't plan on going any faster than the speed limit. Maybe he'd pass her on the next straightaway. All of the rush-hour traffic had cleared, leaving a handful of cars negotiating the turns and bends between Durango and Silverhill.

Coming out of the next turn, Julia buzzed down the window and waved her arm to motion the car around her. She eased off the gas pedal as the car made its move to her left. The sedan pulled into the empty oncoming traffic lane and slowed down next to her.

With her heart galloping, she glanced into the dark car as the driver rolled down the passenger window. A man with black hair and sunglasses leaned toward the open window and yelled. The wind snatched his words, but she could just make out, "Pull over. Flat tire. Lug nuts."

She had a flat tire? The car dropped back and slid in behind her again. Turning down the radio with trembling fingers, she listened for any unusual thumping on the road. Her little car rolled smoothly on the asphalt, taking each turn with ease. How could she have a flat?

Biting her bottom lip, she peered into the rearview mirror at the blue sedan still riding her tail. Was this some kind of trick to get her to pull off the road? Maybe if the guy had a family with him she'd follow his advice, but she didn't have any intention of stopping for some single guy in the middle of the night, especially some single guy wearing sunglasses in the middle of the night. Did he think he was Jack Nicholson or something?

Over the past three years, she'd finally put the freaks and weirdos behind her. She didn't need to go looking for them.

She sped up to put distance between her car and the dark sedan behind her. Her tires squealed as she took the last curve on the highway and her car shuddered in the back. She gasped and squeezed the steering wheel. Maybe she did have a flat.

The light from Ben Pickett's service station glowed at the bottom of the hill, and Julia's pulse slowed to a steady beat. At nine o'clock Ben would still be working.

Careening into the parking lot, she angled her car in front of the brightly lit market. She hunched down in the seat and watched the dark sedan speed past the service station. Either the driver didn't realize she'd stopped or he figured he performed his good deed for the night…or he knew he couldn't strangle her at the service station.

She jumped at the tap on her window. Ben, his cap pulled low on his forehead, grinned at her.

Dragging in a breath, she powered down the window. "Hey, Ben."

"You heading home after class?"

Living in Silverhill, everyone knew her business, but she didn't mind. It gave her a sense of security. At least someone cared about her.

"Yeah, I am. A guy pulled up next to me and yelled out the window that I had a flat tire. The car wobbled when I came off the hill."

"Well, let's have a look." He disappeared as he crouched behind her car and then his head popped up. "The tire ain't flat, but the lug nuts on your right rear wheel are loose. I'll tighten those right up."

Ben got some tools, and Julia ambled into the market to get some coffee. She wrapped her hands around the steaming foam cup as she stepped into the cool night air to watch Ben work. Settling her shoulders against her car door, she gazed into the blackness where the road led into Silverhill. No sign of the dark sedan and the dark-haired man.

Why did he tell her she had a flat tire and how did he know the lug nuts were loose?

Unless he'd loosened them.

JULIA HATED secret admirers.

She crushed the wildflowers in her fist, the petals dropping like tears onto the porch and the sweet smell clinging to her fingers. Someone placed a similar bunch, tied with a pink ribbon, in the same spot two days ago. No note, no name.

Her gaze darted from her fenced-in garden to the street beyond. Nobody lingered to see if she received the gift. Nobody waved, claiming to be the thoughtful neighbor.

Julia hated secrets.

Taking a deep breath, she tilted her head back and drank in the view of tall mountain peaks ringing the cozy town of Silverhill. Their proximity instilled a sense of security deep in her bones. The Colorado Rockies kept the outside world at bay, creating a safe haven for her and her daughter in this little community.

The trees across the road rustled, and Julia narrowed her eyes as she scanned the greenery. The incident with the tire last week had her on edge. She'd asked around and a few people told her a loose wheel could resemble a flat tire on the highway. The man in the car was probably more Good Samaritan than Ted Bundy. But a single woman couldn't be too careful. Especially a single woman with no memory.

She spotted a flash of red clothing zigzagging through the trees and her pulse ticked up a few notches. Tossing the bedraggled bouquet over the porch railing into the dirt, she backed up to her front door and stumbled over the threshold. The screen door slammed and she reached for the door handle.

A woman's voice sang out, "How are you today, Julia?"

Julia peered through the mesh of the screen door, releasing her pent-up breath. Gracie Malone, the town gossip, leaned over her garden fence, waving.

Julia would be damned if she'd have Gracie spreading stories about how she scampered inside her house the minute she saw someone in her front yard.

"I'm just fine, Gracie. Out for an early morning walk?" She shoved the screen door open and wedged her shoulder on the doorjamb.

"Yes, and you? Are you and that adorable little girl of yours going for a hike this morning?" Gracie's bright little eyes, like black buttons, flickered from the beribboned flowers on the ground to Julia's face.

"I'm packing up right now." Or she had been until she noticed the scraggly posies on the porch railing.

"It's such a shame Shelby doesn't have a father." Gracie shook her head back and forth in an exaggerated fashion, her tight gray curls quivering. She tapped her chin. "Charlie's still sweet on you. We have a lot of room in that old Victorian, you know, even with the B and B."

Julia knew Gracie desperately wanted to marry off her only son so she could have more people in the house to boss around and someone to help out with the guests. So desperate she'd saddle her only son with the town freak.

"We're going to get ready for that hike now. You have a good day." Julia left the front door open, settling on locking the screen door. She had more to fear from Gracie Malone and her dull son than some secret admirer. Could that secret admirer be Charlie?

"Mama?" Shelby padded out of her bedroom rubbing her eyes with bunched-up fists.

"Hey, sleepyhead. We're going on a hike this morning." She scooped Shelby into her arms and buried her face in her neck, inhaling the sweet fragrance of watermelon shampoo from her hair. At four, Shelby no longer had that pure baby smell, but new, interesting smells were replacing it. Little girl smells.

Shelby giggled as Julia found her ticklish spot along her collarbone. "I'll help you get dressed."

Twenty minutes later, Julia swung the backpack over her shoulder and locked the front door behind her. Crushing the crumpled flowers into the dirt with her heel, she took Shelby's hand and headed toward the road.

From Silverhill's main street, they picked up the entrance to the mile-long trail that wound its way into the foothills. The trail followed a soft slope, skirting outcroppings of rock and spreading into fields of wildflowers and gentle streams—a perfect outing for a four-year-old and a woman still fighting to regain emotional stability.

Spring had come early to the Rockies and summer was hot on its heels. The early morning sun warmed Julia's face. Shelby slowed the pace by picking up stones, snatching flowers from the rock crevices and veering off the path to chase butterflies.

"Ouch!" A rock bit into Julia's heel. When she stopped to slip off her shoe, Shelby zipped around the next bend. Holding her sneaker, Julia hobbled after her.

"Shelby?" She rounded the corner, but Shelby had disappeared. A swath of anxiety settled on her skin as her gaze raked through the thick patch of trees. Julia plowed forward, rubbing her arms. "Shelby, come back or we're going home right now."

Her mischievous daughter crawled out from behind a log, pinching a worm between two fingers.

"Okay, you can drop that right there." Julia held up her hands, wrinkling her nose at her tomboy daughter.

Shelby placed the worm on the log and waved to it before returning to Julia's side. She grabbed Shelby's wrist and marched her back to the trail. "Stay with me now."

When they got back to the path, a small rock tumbled from above. Glancing up, Julia glimpsed a shadow passing across the face of the cliff. She called out, "Hello?"

A tree rustled and a branch snapped, sending a bird screeching into the sky. She glanced back at the sandy-colored cliffs, tightening her grip on Shelby's wrist. Cupping a hand over her mouth, she breathed in and out slowly to steady her galloping heart. She thought she'd put those panic attacks behind her, but a few crackling twigs and falling rocks could still bring on a racing heart and shallow breathing.

"Run, Mama." Shelby slid out of Julia's clammy grasp and skipped ahead, landing face-down in a patch of bluebells.

"Shelby!" Julia tripped after her, sinking to her knees in the flowers.

Shelby rolled onto her back, covering her face with two small dirty hands. She peeked through her fingers and giggled. A surge of warm relief melted Julia's rigid muscles and she kissed Shelby's butterscotch curls.

"Silly girl. You scared me."

"Mama scared?" Shelby sat up, scooping a handful of bluebells in her fist and dropping them into Julia's lap.

Julia peered into the shadows and crevices of the rocks and shook her head. "No, I'm not scared…anymore."

The fear that had enveloped her when she first found herself in Silverhill had dissipated over the past four years, driven away by friendly neighbors, soothing words and warm suppers. But sometimes it descended on her with no warning, dropping like an anvil in the middle of the night or silently stealing over her, one uneasy moment at a time. Like today.

She twisted her head over her shoulder to study the trail she and Shelby had just traversed. A sense of doom dogged her on the hike, a feeling of being watched and followed. It started with the stranger in the car and picked up with the flowers left on her porch two days ago and then again today. Most women would be thrilled with a secret admirer. She wasn't most women.

The flowers could've come from a neighbor. Julia massaged her temples. And she didn't own this trail. Locals and tourists alike took the mile hike up to the rock formations known as "The Twirling Ballerinas." Anyone could've been hiking behind them.

Why didn't they answer when she called out?

Julia cradled the bluebells in her palms and buried her face in their fresh fragrance. Too bad the flowers weren't forget-me-nots.

Maybe then she could remember who she was, remember Shelby's father, and remember what shadowy menace stalked her.

Shelby's hands, smelling of moist dirt, pulled at Julia's fingers. "Peekaboo."

Smiling, Julia spread her fingers wide. "Peekaboo to you."

Whatever happened in her past, it brought Shelby into her life so it couldn't have been all doom and gloom. Her daughter's laughter acted like a ray of sunshine capable of piercing the solid block of ice, which was all that remained of Julia's memory despite Dr. Jim Brody's best efforts.

Shelby shrieked, "No, peekaboo to you."

"Can anyone play this game?"

Gasping, Julia dropped her hands and pulled Shelby against her body before the intruder's voice registered. Shelby squirmed in her arms, and Julia loosened her grip as Clem Stoker came into view, his shaggy gray eyebrows drawn together over his nose.

Shelby scampered toward Clem and threw her arms around his legs. "Uncle Clem."

Julia swallowed the lump in her throat. Of course Clem

wasn't Shelby's uncle. Shelby didn't have an uncle or a family or a father, at least none that Julia could remember, but Clem treated them like family as did many of the residents of Silverhill after Julia's accident.

"How's my buttercup?" He lifted her up in the air and swung her around, shifting his gaze to Julia. "Are you okay, Julia? I didn't mean to scare you."

"You didn't." She took a deep, shuddering breath. Just when the residents of Silverhill had stopped tiptoeing on eggshells around her, she had to jump at rustling leaves. "Did you just come up the trail behind us?"

"No." Clem hoisted Shelby on his shoulders. "I'm on my way back from The Twirling Ballerinas. Are you headed that way or do you want to hike back to town with me?"

"We'll go back with you." She hated the tremor in her voice. She knew she had a backbone. It came in handy when she recovered from the injuries she sustained from the car wreck and gave birth to Shelby six weeks later amid strangers.

She fingered the gold chain around her neck with *Julia* written in script, the only clue to her identity and a past she couldn't reclaim, not even with the help of a hypnotist in Denver, Dr. Jim, her psychologist in Durango, and local media coverage.

She stopped her search when the marriage proposals started pouring in and strange people cropped up to claim her as family.

A sense of dread smothered her each time someone called professing to be her husband, mother, sister or fiancé. She knew in her heart she didn't want her past to find her. The car accident hadn't caused her black eye.

"Come on then." Clem extended his weather-beaten hand to her, and she gripped it. "Good thing I came along. You're too frail to carry Shelby back, and I think she's getting tired."

"I'm not frail," Julia snapped and then covered her mouth.

"I didn't mean it like that, honey." Clem patted her shoulder. "You've got more gumption than most men twice your size, but you don't have much meat on your bones and this little lady is getting bigger every day."

He tickled Shelby's calf, and she plowed her heel into his chest.

"Shelby, be careful. If you want to ride on Clem's shoulders, sit still."

Clem laughed. "See what I mean? She's a rambunctious buttercup."

Shelby loved the word and repeated "bumptious, bumptious, bumptious," each time Clem bounced her on his shoulders.

By the time they reached the end of the trail, which spilled onto Silverhill's main street, they were all singing a made-up song about bumptious buttercups. Julia took deep, cleansing breaths of the mountain air, stuffing her previous panic on the dusty shelf of her former life.

They rounded a corner onto the street, and a tall man in jeans and a white cowboy hat glanced up after smacking the back of another man getting into a car.

Julia's pulse ticked up a notch. Strangers. She pulled in a breath and rolled her shoulders back. Tourists.

"Lordy, lordy." Clem stopped beside her, giving Shelby one last bounce on his shoulders. "Look who the cat dragged in. You look like hell, boy."

If that tall, rangy man with the wide shoulders and tight jeans looked like hell, send her straight to the devil. She grinned at her visceral response to the stranger. It had been a long time since she felt that gut-wrenching lust for a man.

"Sorry, Julia." Clem covered Shelby's ears a little too late.

The man took a step forward, his mouth hanging open, his

eyes wide. His tanned face blanched and he reached forward with an unsteady hand.

He looked like he was seeing a ghost…and he was staring right at her.

THROUGH THE ROARING in his ears, Ryder McClintock heard Clem's voice saying his name, but he couldn't respond. All his muscles seized up and his feet felt rooted to the ground.

A crease formed between Julia's eyebrows and she tilted her head to the side, long brown hair sliding across her shoulder. She had different hair and different clothes, but unless he was in the middle of a dream, Julia Rousseau stood before him in the flesh.

"Ryder, what's the matter?" Clem ambled forward and shook his hand, slapping him on the back. Then he reached up to steady the little girl on his shoulders. "You been away so long, the altitude got to you?"

The fog lifted and pinpricks of excitement raced up his spine. She had come to him. Julia had come to him.

"Julia, you're here." Ryder twisted away from Clem and reached for her.

Stumbling back, Julia put her hands up. "Who are you?"

Her words punched him in the gut and he nearly doubled over. Was this some kind of game? Did she want to punish him for leaving her? She, more than anyone, knew he had no choice.

"Julia, it's me, Ryder. Why didn't you write to me? Why didn't you answer my letters?"

Clem choked and grabbed his shoulder. "Are you telling me you know Julia?"

Ryder swiveled his head around. Clem regarded him with the same open-mouthed astonishment that Ryder had bestowed on Julia. Didn't Julia tell the residents of Silverhill that she knew him?

"What the hell is going on?" Ryder shook his head and

swept off his hat. His gaze darted between Julia and Clem, and he plowed his fingers through his hair. "Didn't you tell them?"

The blankness of her face pierced his heart. She didn't recognize him. Three and a half years, and she didn't recognize him. Something else in her expression twisted the dagger even deeper—panic. Julia feared him.

"Don't you recognize me? Ryder McClintock." He felt like a fool introducing himself to the woman he loved with a burning, searing passion—even when he thought she'd deserted him. He took another step forward, and she took a matching step back.

"Ryder." Clem gripped his arm. "Julia doesn't know you. She lost her memory over three years ago when her car took a dive off Highway 160."

Clem's words sucked the air out of Ryder's lungs and a vice squeezed his chest. He searched Julia's face for a glimmer of recognition, for the smile that used to curve her lip, when he told bad jokes, the light in her eyes. Nothing. Worse than nothing—wariness, doubt…fear.

If she didn't recognize him, how'd she wind up here? She must have been coming to him, or rather his family, when she had that accident. What compelled her to seek sanctuary with his family? Did she know about Jeremy?

"I—I, Julia may not know me," he dug the heels of his hands into his eyes to blot out Julia's look of bafflement, "but I know Julia."

Clem laughed and did a little jig in the street. "That's a miracle, Julia. Do you know who Ryder is? He's Ralph's boy come home. You must've been coming to see Ryder when your car took that tumble. Now you can get your life back all right and tight."

Ryder shifted his gaze to Julia, twisting her hands in front of her. She didn't look happy about the prospect of getting her life back.

"I don't get it." Ryder rubbed his knuckles along his jaw. "Didn't Julia have any ID on her? Didn't the police check the registration on the car?"

"Let's not talk about this in the middle of the street." Clem shifted the little girl on his shoulders. "We'll go back to my place and Millie can make us some lunch. She still makes the best lemonade in Silverhill, Ryder."

Clem's granddaughter whinnied and patted Clem on the head. "Let's go. Ride 'em, cowboy."

The tightness of Julia's face smoothed out a little. She must know his family. Who didn't know the McClintocks in Silverhill? They practically ran the town. Ryder took a deep breath. This might not be so bad. How could it be when he'd found Julia again?

Ryder smiled at the little girl. "Another granddaughter, Clem? Has to be Maddy's with those blond curls."

Clem swung the girl off his shoulders. "No, not one of mine. This here's Julia's daughter."

The smile froze on Ryder's face as he gritted his teeth. The girl ran to Julia and wrapped her arms around her legs, smiling shyly at him over her shoulder.

She must be about four years old, and if his guess was right…she belonged to him.

Chapter Two

Clem filled the stranger's ears with local gossip as they ambled toward his house, covering the awkwardness that hung in the air like one of those heavy Native American blankets sold from roadside campers.

The truth of her past hovered right around the corner and she didn't know whether to laugh or cry. Perhaps this stranger...no, Ryder McClintock...didn't know her that well. Wouldn't his family have recognized her name as one of Ryder's friends? Of course, they knew only her first name.

His father and stepmother didn't mention him often and he hadn't been to visit them in over three years. She recalled talk of the McClintocks' middle boy working overseas on some kind of a secret mission. How did she know a spy? Perhaps they had some brief acquaintance.

If she didn't know him well, why was she on her way to see him that fateful night when her car skidded off the road in a snowstorm? That couldn't be a coincidence. She must've been seeking out Ryder when she crashed, but where had he been the past three years?

As Ryder chatted with Clem, his responses terse, he avoided looking at her but seemed fascinated by Shelby. Julia's heart skittered in her chest. He could probably tell her all about Shelby's father, where he was and why he never came looking for them.

"Hat, please." Shelby strained away from Julia's tight grip, leaning toward Ryder.

"You want my hat?" Ryder grinned down at Shelby, a gleam lighting his blue eyes.

"I'm sorry. Everyone spoils her around here." She tugged Shelby back to her side. "Don't be rude, Shelby."

"Her name's Shelby?" Ryder shoved his hands into his tight blue jeans. "That was my grandmother's name."

"I know. Ralph, your father, told me that after I named her." She folded her arms, gripping her elbows. "Do you think…?"

"Hat." Shelby stomped her feet before planting them firmly on the dirt road.

"Young lady," Julia crouched next to her, "I'm going to tell Aunt Millie not to give you any sugar cookies unless you behave yourself." She secretly thanked her daughter for the distraction. After almost four years of having a blank slate for a memory, she didn't think she could handle someone filling up that slate too quickly.

Julia looked up at the man who held the key to her identity and rolled her eyes. "She's stubborn."

"Just like…" Ryder stopped and clenched his jaw. Then he lifted his hat from his head and placed it on Shelby's. "There you go, a real Colorado cowgirl."

Shelby squealed and holding her hands in front of her as if gripping reins, she trotted around the three adults, as the hat slid down to her nose.

"Thanks, but you didn't have to do that." Julia stood up next to Ryder as a breeze lifted the ends of his brown hair, touched with gold. She flinched at the pain lurking in his eyes and it took a physical effort for her not to reach up and smooth her palms across the creases at the sides of his mouth.

She couldn't be Ryder McClintock's wife. His family would've known if he had a wife. Ryder could give her a husband and a father for Shelby, it just wouldn't be him. Her throat tightened and tears pricked behind her eyes.

Her knees trembled at her response to this tall, broad-shouldered man—the McClintocks' son. She slipped her arm through Clem's, leaning on his shoulder.

"R-Ryder and I have to talk, Clem."

"I know that, honey." He patted her shoulder. "Let's just make it back to my place, and Millie will get some lunch for Shelby and you two can have some privacy."

Clem's neat ranch house appeared all too soon. His wife, Millie, waved from the porch, a dish towel in her hand. She called out, "I heard Ryder was back in town. How'd you get him first?"

"Just luck." Clem strode to the porch as fast as his old bones could carry him and mumbled something to Millie.

Julia overheard her name, Ryder's name, and something about her memory. Word would spread as fast as a Colorado brushfire. It always did.

"Mercy me." Millie covered her mouth with the dish towel, her eyes wide above it. She scurried down the steps and stood on tiptoe to plant a kiss on Ryder's cheek. "I hope you can help our Julia."

Clem grabbed Shelby's hand. "C'mon, buttercup, cookies and lemonade for you after lunch and then I'll take you out to see Missycat's kittens."

Millie placed a plump arm around Julia's shoulders. "You and Ryder can have the patio out back. Plenty of privacy there."

Julia's stomach churned and she stumbled on the top step.

Ryder placed a steadying hand against the small of her back, beneath her backpack, his warmth seeping through the thin cotton of her T-shirt. Her hyperawareness of him had to be due to their connection in her previous life.

She always referred to her past as her previous life, as if it had no bearing on the life she led in Silverhill. The foolish phrase allowed her to ignore the terror she always felt when she groped in the shadowy darkness of her past for answers. Now a collision between her past and present loomed before her. Was she ready for the fallout?

"Behave yourself and don't be greedy." Julia settled Shelby at the Stokers' kitchen table, while Millie handed Ryder two glasses of lemonade.

Ryder led the way to the patio and Julia followed, her gaze clinging to his tight jeans molded to his behind—a pleasant distraction from the uncertainty that lurked around the corner.

Too bad Ryder didn't rush in claiming to be her long-lost husband like so many others had. She might have accepted Ryder's story without question.

He clicked the glasses down on the glass-topped table, and then pulled out her chair. The legs scraping against the flagstone jarred her from her pleasant reverie back to the present…back to the past. She perched on the edge of the chair and wrapped her hands around the sweating glass.

Settling beside her, Ryder sipped his lemonade and then turned his blue eyes to her. His gaze meandered over her face and hair and skimmed her shoulders. A sinuous warmth suffused her skin, his intimate inventory feeling like a caress.

"You look…different."

"Let's cut to the chase, Ryder." She rubbed her damp palms on the thighs of her jeans. "Who am I?"

A quick grin split his face. "Not so different after all."

His smile took her breath away, and she gripped the edge of the table to keep from sliding beneath it. Damn, if this man wasn't her husband in her previous life, she must've had a hot fling with him. Or should have.

"Okay." He planted his hands on his knees. "Your name is Julia Scott, although after you and Jeremy separated you started using your maiden name, Rousseau. How'd you remember your first name?"

"Wait a minute." A dull pain thumped behind her eyes as she held up her hands. "You're going too fast. I'm divorced?"

Dragging in a breath, Ryder raked a hand through his thick brown hair and the sun glinted off the golden streaks. "I'm sorry. I guess I'm not very good at filling in someone about her life. You were married to Jeremy Scott for less than a year. Things didn't go so well after he got back from Afghanistan, and you split up."

"Afghanistan? My husband was in the military?" Maybe the military deployed him again, and that's why he never looked for her.

"Yeah." Ryder shifted his gaze and took a long swallow of lemonade.

"And my parents? My family? Why didn't anyone else look for me?" She held her breath as she watched Ryder trace beads of moisture on the glass with his fingertip.

"I don't think you have close family in the States, Julia. Your father, Girard Rousseau, was a diplomat with the U.S. Embassy in France. He passed away about five years ago. As far as I know, your mother, Celeste Rousseau, still lives in Paris." A smile quirked the edge of his mouth. "And you and your mom were never close. When I called her, she said the two of you had had a falling out. She hadn't seen or heard from you in years and figured you'd headed out for parts unknown."

Yeah and who would figure those unknown parts would be her own mind? She slumped back in her chair and exhaled. Her father was dead. Her estranged mother lived in Paris. Her ex-husband was probably fighting overseas.

That explained the deafening silence when she tried to search for her identity. She clasped her hands in her lap. It didn't explain her black eye or what she was doing in a stolen car with mounds of cash in the trunk and no ID.

Ryder's large hand covered hers and his warmth soaked into her bones. "I'm sorry this happened to you, Julia. Didn't you have any ID? Whose car were you driving?"

She met his gaze. His touch, his presence calmed her, making her feel as secure as those mountains that ringed her world for the past three and a half years.

"I didn't have a purse, a suitcase or any identification with me. I was driving a stolen car. The police found the owner of the car in Washington, but he didn't know me. Th-there was a lot of money in a bag in the backseat of the car, but the owner didn't know anything about it. The police held on to the money for almost a year, tried to trace the serial numbers and then released it to me. It totaled about three hundred thousand dollars."

His glittering blue eyes narrowed and he squeezed her hands before releasing them. "That's a lot of money."

"Why would I have that much money?"

"Your mom's rich." He lifted a shoulder, but his face tightened as if she'd transferred her anxiety to him.

"And the stolen car?"

"Did the police charge you with any crime?" he asked.

"No, they put it down to a mystery in my past, besides I was injured and pregnant. The owner of the car didn't want to press any charges."

"God, I wish I could've been there for you." Ryder jumped up from his chair, knocking it to the ground.

His concern caused her heart to thump against her rib cage. He knew her…Julia Rousseau Scott…and he cared about her. That knowledge gave her strength, the strength to examine her past and unveil its secrets.

She took a deep breath. "How did you know me? It seems as if I didn't have any friends who cared about me enough to search for me."

"Oh, you had lots of friends." He stopped pacing and shoved a hand in his pocket. "In Paris. I heard you'd followed Jeremy to Tucson, but if you landed here almost four years ago I don't think you had time to form a circle of friends in Arizona."

"You knew me in Paris?" Her voice squeaked. Even though she'd discovered she knew French last week, she never imagined she'd lived in Paris.

"That's where I met you. I worked with… Jeremy and I served in the same unit. When I came to Paris on leave, Jeremy introduced me to his new wife."

Ryder worked with her ex-husband? Did this mean her ex-husband was a spy, too? Did Jeremy even know about her pregnancy, about his daughter? Would she have to share Shelby with a stranger? Her gut clenched. She didn't want to share Shelby with anyone.

Running her hands across her face as if brushing away cobwebs, she pushed out of her chair. "Where is he? Where's Jeremy?"

Ryder spun around and gripped her shoulders. "Jeremy's dead."

She closed her eyes and waited for the grief, the sharp pang of regret, a twist of guilt. Nothing. She felt nothing but a flare of relief. No stranger would be knocking on her door to take Shelby for court-mandated visits with a father she didn't know.

"Are you okay?" Ryder squeezed her shoulders.

Her eyes flew open. With his face inches from hers, she could smell his strong, clean scent and the citrus on his breath from the fresh lemonade. Two lines formed on either side of his mouth and his nostrils flared. Did he expect her to collapse?

"I—I don't feel anything. I know he was your friend, but all I feel is relief that he can't take my daughter. Am I a horrible person? I'm sorry you lost your friend." A sob escaped her lips for the man, Shelby's father, she'd never know.

The pressure on her shoulders turned to a caress and Ryder pulled her into an embrace. She molded against his hard body, and he tightened his arms around her, laying his cheek on the top of her head. Her blood sang in her veins as she rested against the solid comfort of his chest.

He murmured against her hair, "You're not a horrible person. Your reaction is natural. You don't remember Jeremy. How could you feel anything about the news of his death?"

Julia curled her arms around Ryder's waist. Maybe if Jeremy stood here on the Stokers' patio, holding her in his arms, she'd remember. The strong connection she felt with Ryder bubbled up from somewhere in her subconscious. Dr. Jim always believed if she met someone from her past, memories would start to return.

The memories still remained blank, but the feeling she had for Ryder surged through her, real and strong. She turned her head and pressed her lips against the warm skin of his throat, moving her hips against his. His breath hissed between his teeth, and she jumped back, disentangling herself from his embrace and the confusing feelings swirling in her head.

"I—I'm sorry." She covered her face with her hands to hide the hot flash that claimed her cheeks.

"You don't have anything to be sorry about. This must be…" He placed his hand on her back and steered her back to her chair. "Sit."

She dropped into the chair, and Ryder shoved her glass of lemonade in front of her. She gulped the cool liquid and then pressed the glass against her hot face. Ryder must think she'd lost her mind along with her memory, coming onto him right after learning about her dead husband…ex-husband.

"How did Jeremy die and when?" She had to start piecing together the string of events in her past life that led to her accident in a stolen car with a bag of cash.

"You were living in Paris when Jeremy finished his last assignment." He cocked his head. "Do you know that you speak French like a native?"

"Yeah, I discovered that just last week."

Shaking his head, he said, "Weird."

"You don't know the half of weird. Go on."

"You worked as a tour guide at the Louvre. Anyway, Jeremy returned from the field, and you two fought and decided to separate."

"After one fight?" Her marriage to Jeremy couldn't have been that strong.

"One of many fights." Ryder shrugged his broad shoulders. "Jeremy left his job and went out to Tucson. When I found out about Jeremy's…death, I called you in Paris. That's when I learned you went to the States, but I don't know why you followed him."

"I was with him when he died?" She swallowed the uneasy lump in her throat.

"I don't know, Julia. I saw you last in Paris before I left for my next assignment." He shifted his gaze from hers and stared across the Stokers' back yard that stretched into a paddock for their horses. "When I heard about Jeremy I called you, but you were gone. When I got back to Paris, I looked for you again, but you'd disappeared. I didn't see you again until today."

"You didn't answer my question, Ryder." Wings of anxiety fluttered in her belly. Something didn't add up about Ryder's story. He said Jeremy was in Afghanistan, in the military, but he talked of assignments instead of deployment. And what American soldier lived in Paris? The McClintocks never mentioned their son being in the armed services. He worked for a government agency, some said the CIA.

"How did Jeremy die?"

"Julia, we don't have to go into this right now. You must be on overload. There's plenty of time to get into this stuff, and I'll be around for a while."

"Before you get your next assignment?" She crossed her arms, squelching all the squishy feelings she had about this man. She needed some answers. "What agency do you work for?"

Leaning back in his chair, he stretched his long legs in front of him. His worn cowboy boots looked right at home on the dusty roads that led from Silverhill to the ranches that surrounded it. Of course he fit in because his family owned one of the biggest ranches, but he was also at home in Paris, Afghanistan, and wherever else he'd been hiding out these past three and a half years.

"I can't tell you that."

"Or you'd have to kill me?" Her own attempt at humor caused a chill to ripple down her spine. Hunching her shoulders, she gripped her upper arms. "I must've known at some point because I was married to one of your coworkers."

"You knew a little, but it's best for those memories to stay buried."

"Damn you." She banged her fist on the table, and the ice

in the glasses tinkled and shook. "You're not the gatekeeper of my memories. Did Jeremy's death have anything to do with this top secret agency? Is it the reason I was fleeing in a stolen car with gobs of cash?"

"I don't know."

"Liar."

A quick grin broke across his face. "Still as hot-tempered as ever."

She was? Nobody in Silverhill had ever accused her of having a hot temper. They tiptoed around sweet, gentle Julia and spoke in hushed voices so as not to startle her. She hated it.

Ryder sat forward and traced a finger along the knuckles of her clenched fist. "You never told me how you knew your name was Julia."

A blatant attempt to change the subject, but his warm touch somehow made that okay. Not wanting to break away from him, Julia plucked her necklace from beneath her T-shirt with her other hand. Hooking her thumb behind the gold script of her name, she pulled it forward.

Ryder took it from her and ran the tip of his finger along the letters. Her heart ached at the gentle way he caressed her name. His eyes crinkled and a smile tugged at his lips.

"Do you recognize it?" She held her breath.

"Yeah, you wore it all the time."

His eyes met hers, and she shivered at the longing mirrored in their depths. She shared a past with this man. His lips, inches from hers, invited her to explore further. As much as she wanted to, she had to learn more about herself, about her dead husband, Shelby's father.

The patio door slid open, and Shelby barreled across the bricks and threw herself into Julia's lap. "I want to go home. Uncle Clem said I could have a kitty."

"Okay, we can go home now, but we have to wait until the kitties are ready to leave their mama." Julia glanced at Ryder, who was smiling down at Shelby.

Shelby turned her head, a quick grin splitting her face. "I have your hat."

"Then let's go get it." Ryder tweaked one of Shelby's curls before he stood up. "And I'll walk you and your mama home."

Millie collected the glasses from the table, her gaze darting between Julia and Ryder. "You learn anything, honey?"

"Yeah, but we have a lot more to discuss."

Ryder raised his brows, but before he could utter a word, Shelby grabbed his hand, tugging him toward the house. With narrowed eyes, Julia watched her daughter pull the handsome stranger inside. Seemed Ryder McClintock had cast a spell over her daughter, too.

As Julia and Ryder sauntered down the dirt road to her house, Shelby skipped ahead of them, examining every rock and stick along the way.

"She's really bright and talkative."

"She was my lifeline after the accident." Tears pricked her eyes and she dashed them away. "Does she look anything like Jeremy?"

Ryder stiffened beside her and lifted a shoulder. "I think she looks like you."

"Was I pregnant when Jeremy and I divorced?" It bothered her that she'd separate from her husband when they were going to have a child together.

Her house came into view, and Shelby pushed through the front gate.

"I didn't know anything about your pregnancy." Ryder kicked at some pebbles on the road. "You weren't pregnant the last time I saw you in Paris…before I left on assignment."

"Were Jeremy and I separated at that point?" She gnawed

at her bottom lip, trying to piece together the strands of her life, like a movie where she knew the ending and had to figure out the beginning and the middle.

"Yes." A muscle twitched in his jaw.

"Mama, more flowers." Shelby ran back toward the road, clutching a bunch of wildflowers tied with a blue ribbon.

Julia's heart pounded as she took the bouquet of flowers from her daughter. Two offerings in one day? Her secret admirer had just turned up the heat.

"Is anything wrong?" Ryder's brow furrowed as he tilted his head.

"Someone has been leaving me flowers the past few weeks." She shrugged with a nonchalance she didn't feel. "A secret admirer."

"You used to love flowers...roses." He pushed the gate open for her. "That's how Jeremy proposed to you. He filled your apartment in Paris with roses."

"What an extravagant gesture. How'd it all go downhill from a rose-filled proposal?"

"You inspired extravagant gestures."

"Me?" She laughed. "Now I inspire scraggly bouquets of wildflowers."

She shoved her key in the door, pushing it open. Many residents of Silverhill left their doors unlocked, especially during the day, but she never felt safe doing that. Maybe once she reclaimed her past, she'd stop looking over her shoulder, even though that past according to Ryder McClintock still contained secrets and unanswered riddles.

"Does Shelby take a nap? If you're not on overload, we can continue talking. I can tell you about the time you jumped in the fountain fully clothed and the other time when you inspired a skinny-dipping session at a party."

"You're kidding."

"I am not." His blue eyes gleamed with a wicked light. "I was at the party."

Shelby danced around Ryder's legs. "Come see my rock collection."

"You can show Ryder your collection, and then it's time for a nap." She had a lot to learn about herself, that carefree, uninhibited woman…and a lot to learn about Ryder.

Julia slid the backpack off her shoulder and pushed open her bedroom door. She stopped at the threshold and grabbed the doorjamb for support.

The blood rushed to her head and the roaring in her ears drowned out the sound of her own scream as it ripped through her throat.

Chapter Three

Ryder dropped the shiny piece of obsidian and lurched to his feet. Shelby clutched his fingers, and he swept her up in his arms. He charged into the small hallway where Julia sagged against her bedroom door.

"What is it?" He shifted Shelby to his left arm, wrapping his right around Julia's waist. She leaned against his body and pointed a shaking finger toward her bed.

Bits and pieces of shredded material lay scattered across the chintz coverlet. A pair of scissors extended from the middle of the mattress.

"Mama's underwear." Shelby squirmed out of his arms and scampered toward the mess on the bed.

"Shelby!" Julia shouted and yanked her daughter back. "Leave it alone. I—I forgot I left my underwear here this morning."

She turned pleading eyes toward him, and when could he ever resist Julia Rousseau anything? Taming the rage that burned in his belly for the unknown intruder who just destroyed Julia's peace, Ryder scooped up Shelby. "Why don't you get a tea party ready for me in your room?"

By the time he settled Shelby in her bedroom and scoured the rest of the small house, he returned to Julia's bedroom where she crouched beside the bed, fingering the remnants of lacy bras and silk panties.

"Don't touch anything, Julia. Leave it for the police."

Her hand trembled as she dropped the material and then she covered her face. He'd never seen Julia show weakness before and her fear punched him in the gut. What kind of maniacs were running around Silverhill these days? If, in fact, a Silverhill local played this sick joke.

Dropping to his knees beside her, he wrapped her in a tight embrace. He smoothed her long, silky hair with his palm and inhaled her fresh, sweet scent, which resembled those wildflowers she'd tossed on the coffee table. "Do you have any idea who did this? Could it be a stupid prank?"

She shook her head, burrowing deeper against his chest.

"It's probably connected to those flowers." It looked like Julia had a stalker who just graduated from innocent gifts of flowers to more sinister acts of intimacy. He'd returned home to Silverhill just in time to protect her.

Just like he'd protected her from Jeremy.

"I think it is." She rubbed her nose on his shirt and pulled away from him. "I got the first bouquet two weeks ago, a second one last week, and two today. There was one on my porch this morning before we left on our hike."

"What did you do with all of them?"

"I threw them away, except for the one this morning. I got sick of it and crushed the flowers into the dirt."

He smoothed the hair from her brow. He wanted to kiss her, but held back. He had to give her some time before telling her about their relationship…and Shelby.

The little girl had to be his unless Julia and Jeremy indulged in some postseparation sex, and Julia would have never done that. She'd loved him as much as he loved her, still loved her.

Somehow he had to win her love back, but he had a feeling he wouldn't do it with secrets. And he couldn't just charge back into her life and take what rightfully belonged to him. He had that little girl to consider now. He had to protect her, too.

He shook his head. "Seems your stalker saw the abandoned flowers and got pissed off."

"Stalker?" A tremble rolled through her slight frame, and he silently cursed himself. He wanted to treat this intrusion lightly for her sake, brush it off as a harmless prank.

This Julia with her broken memories and tentative hold on a new life didn't have the same strength as the old Julia, who routinely battled with her mother and kicked her cheating spouse to the curb.

"Maybe he's just a harmless, love-struck fool." He rubbed her back.

Tilting her chin toward the scissors, she said, "That doesn't look harmless to me. How'd he get into my home?"

On his inspection of her house he noticed the back door slightly ajar, but he didn't want to touch anything. "He may have broken in through the back. Let's get the police over here. I know Will Ballard is still the sheriff because my brother, Rafe, works for him, but Rafe's in the Academy since he transferred over from L.A. Who else is on the force?"

"Ballard's son, Zack, works with him, too."

He rolled his eyes, keeping the mood light. "Lord, save us from Zack Ballard."

That earned him a snort and his heart clutched. Julia didn't giggle. She snorted and then the snorts turned into big belly laughs that had everyone joining in. He wanted that woman back…although, this new Julia had a softness about her the old Julia would've scorned, and his retro-caveman side found it damned attractive.

The old Julia never wanted children either, but Ryder could tell Julia was a loving mother. Did she reconsider the idea of kids because she'd been carrying his baby? Why didn't she tell him, and why did she go to Jeremy in Arizona? Did she even get a chance to see Jeremy before he died?

He couldn't give her all her memories and didn't know if he wanted to give her the bad ones. Of course she never told him about her pregnancy. He hadn't wanted children, either.

He'd always shied away from commitments for just that reason. After the disaster of his parents' marriage and his role in breaking apart his family, he didn't want one of his own. Didn't deserve one of his own.

Fifteen minutes later with Shelby sound asleep, the father-son team of Will and Zack Ballard showed up at Julia's house. Ryder figured Will would've retired by now, but maybe he didn't feel comfortable letting his bumbling son out on the streets without his guidance. Or he figured the new sheriff would fire Zack.

"Good to see you back, Ryder." Zack crushed Ryder's hand with his massive paw. "Are you going to stick around this time or do you have another secret assignment coming up?"

Ryder squeezed back until Zack blinked his eyes and struggled out of his grip. Zack always had to prove himself, and he did it with a pumped-up physique and a macho swagger.

"Can't tell you that, Zack. That's why it's called a secret assignment." Ryder winked to take out the sting of his words. He could understand Zack's effort to escape the shadow of a larger-than-life father.

Ryder's own father, Ralph, controlled his ranch and his family with an iron hand. It was one of the reasons Ryder took a job with the CIA—the top secret stuff came later when he joined the covert ops division, Black Cobra…and met Jeremy Scott.

"You look good, boy." Will pounded him on the back while he shook his hand. He drew his bushy brows over his nose. "I heard you know Julia."

"I'd forgotten how fast word travels in this town." Ryder glanced at Julia, who was biting her luscious lower lip. He wanted to protect her from the small-town gossip mill, but she'd probably had a starring role these past few years. This new trouble would only add to her fame.

"Is he clearing things up for you?" Will patted Julia's shoulder.

"A few things." She compressed her lips, and Ryder knew he hadn't escaped her tough questions.

"Let's get down to business." Zack crossed his arms over his pumped-up chest. "A perp broke into Julia's house? Should we seal off the crime scene, Pop…I mean Sheriff Ballard?"

Ryder knew he could count on Zach for some comic relief. He shot a quick look at Julia and her dancing eyes met his as the corner of her mouth twitched. He couldn't allow her to snort at Zack and destroy his manhood, so he grabbed Zack's arm and spun him around toward the hallway. "I don't know if you need to seal off the crime scene, but I'll take you to the evidence."

"What's all this?" Zack stood in the center of Julia's bedroom, cocking his head, a furrow between his brows.

"It's my underwear, and the scissors some maniac used to cut it up." Julia waved her arm at the bed, and then pointed to her open dresser drawer. "He got everything out of that drawer. Ryder and I didn't touch anything in case he left fingerprints."

Will pulled out two pairs of gloves from his briefcase and tossed one set to Zack, who'd dropped to his knees by the side of the bed.

Zack snapped on the gloves and his Adam's apple bobbed as he ran his hands through Julia's sliced-up lingerie. It thrilled Ryder that beneath her jeans and T-shirt Julia still had a fondness of sexy lingerie, but that didn't mean he wanted some other man to get a thrill out of it.

"The scissors, Zack. Maybe he left prints." Ryder kneed Zack in the back.

Zack reddened to the roots of his receding hairline. He plucked the scissors from the mattress and then dropped them in the plastic bag his father held out for him.

The Ballards dusted the rest of the room for prints, including the ransacked dresser drawer, but came up empty. Ryder showed them the back door. The intruder hadn't left any prints there either, but he had jimmied the lock.

"Do you have another evidence bag for this?" Julia held up the flowers by the end of the yellow ribbon. "It was on my porch when we got home. There was another one this morning, but it's gone, and I threw away the other two I got in the past two weeks."

"Looks like you got yourself a secret admirer, Julia. The flowers and the scene in the bedroom are obviously connected." Will took the bouquet from Julia and dropped it into another plastic bag.

Julia hunched her shoulders. "The flowers were one thing, but why did he get violent?"

"Probably because you didn't show proper appreciation for the offering this morning." Ryder draped an arm around Julia, and turned to Will. "Julia stomped on the flowers the guy left this morning."

"Seems like overkill to me." Will jerked his thumb toward the bedroom. "Anyone ask you on a date, Julia? Someone you turned down?"

Leaning against Ryder, Julia shook her head. "N-no."

Ryder clenched his jaw. Was she lying? Why would she lie to protect someone? Julia had been loyal to a fault. Her girlfriends in Paris tried to warn her about Jeremy's cheating ways, but Julia shrugged them off. Until she walked in on the evidence.

Will grabbed his hat. "Get that lock fixed, and I know you always do, but keep your doors locked. Be aware of your surroundings and be careful going to and from that night class in Durango."

Julia jerked beneath his arm, and Ryder slid a gaze to her face, which paled. "Anything else?"

Gripping her hands in front of her, Julia told them about the driver of a dark sedan trying to get her to pull over on the highway and the loose lug nuts on her wheel.

"Do you think he might have something to do with the break-in?" Her gaze darted between the three men, settling on Will.

"Maybe. Did you get a good look at the driver?" Will took a spiral notebook out of his pocket and scribbled a few notes.

"No. It was dark. He was wearing sunglasses, which was weird, and he had black hair, but it could've been brown." Julia glanced at Ryder's hair.

Great. Did she suspect him?

"Just be careful." Will shoved his notebook back in his pocket. "We'll run the scissors and the ribbons for fingerprints. Doesn't help that we're at the beginning of the summer tourist season. The hotels, B and B's and dude ranches are already filling up, and we have plenty of strangers in town."

"I'll make sure she stays safe." Ryder clasped Julia's hands, still wound tightly in front of her.

Will's brows shot up and Julia stepped back, snatching her hands away from Ryder.

Zack cleared his throat. "Don't tell me you're married to Julia, too."

Will elbowed his son in the ribs. "Let's get going, Zack. I'm sure Ryder and Julia have a lot to discuss outside of all this mess. We'll let you know if we find anything, Julia."

When the Ballards left, Julia peeked in on Shelby and then returned to the scene of the crime to sift through her shredded lingerie.

Ryder propped a shoulder on the door. "Anything salvageable?"

"Not much." Perching on the edge of the bed, she held up two pieces of a bra, snipped in half.

His gut twisted and he dug his shoulder into the doorjamb to keep from rushing across the room and taking her in his arms. Did this attack have anything to do with her past? He owed her the truth. She'd be safer knowing the truth.

"Zack's an idiot, but did you have a lot of men coming out of the woodwork claiming to be your husband?"

Julia fell back on the bed and stared at the ceiling. "Yeah. The local papers ran my story and scores of people stepped forward to claim me." Her hands clawed at the remnants of her underwear.

"I felt sorry for most of them seeking runaway daughters, missing wives, lost sisters. They all came looking for something. They all wanted me to be someone."

A cold fear cinched the back of his neck. Any of those imposters could've fooled her. "How did you rule them out?"

"They had to have proof." She scooped up the silky material and let it fall on top of her like giant, colorful snowflakes. "And nobody had it."

"Have you tried to regain your memory?"

"Yep—first a hypnotist and then a psychologist. I'm still working on it. I see Dr. Brody in Durango once a week. He's a hypnotist, too, but that didn't work for me."

"Is he helping at all? Have you had any glimmers of memories?"

She sat up, clutching the shredded underwear to her chest. "Not until today."

"You mean my telling you about your past triggered some memories?" He held his breath, his heart thumping painfully against his rib cage.

"No. You did."

"What does that mean?"

"You." She jumped up and the silky material slid from her body, pooling on the floor. "Just being near you makes me feel..."

She remembered. Ryder took a step forward, but Julia held her hands out, palms forward. The gesture sliced him like a sharp blade. He had to give her time. He had to give Shelby time. Would this new Julia fall in love with him all over again?

"Tell me about Jeremy. How did I meet him?"

He clenched his jaw. He didn't want to talk about her and Jeremy and their ill-fated relationship, but he represented her only link to her past right now and she deserved to get that back. Warts and all.

"Like I mentioned, you worked as a tour guide at the Louvre. Jeremy worked for the same organization as I do, a covert branch of the CIA, and he went to Paris between assignments."

Her brown eyes widened. "I was married to a spy? How did we meet?"

"Where a lot of couples meet, at a party."

She sawed at her bottom lip, a small crease between her brows. "Did I party a lot?"

Not only did Julia party a lot, she was the life of every party she attended. Her wild behavior and expensive tastes attracted a merry band of revelers willing to follow her anywhere.

"Well?"

Ryder glanced at the woman before him, her hands shoved into a pair of faded jeans, a smudge of dirt on the shoulder of her cheap T-shirt.

"Yeah, you did. Your father had passed away the year before and I think most of your…hijinks…came from grief. Anyway, you and Jeremy hit it off and got married a few months later."

"Short courtship, no wonder it ended in divorce." She scuffed the toe of her tennis shoe against the carpet. "Were you at that party?"

"No." If he had been there, Jeremy never would've had a chance with Julia.

"The marriage must've gone downhill pretty quickly."

"I'm sorry, Julia. Jeremy cheated on you, and you found out the hard way."

She shrugged. "It's not as if I remember the guy, but it's not easy to hear that Shelby's father was a cheat."

Ryder licked his dry lips. She needed more time. Maybe she'd remember on her own. "Is this ringing any bells?"

"It resounds here." She clenched her fist and tapped her chest above her heart. "When I started looking for my identity, I had the feeling I didn't want to find my husband. I wanted to stay lost. Now I know why."

"Yeah, but we still don't know why you followed him to Arizona."

"A package." Julia gasped and pressed her fingers to her temples.

"What?" Ryder's head jerked up. "Do you remember something?"

Sinking to the bed, Julia massaged her head. "I just had a flash of memory—a picture of a small flat package wrapped in white paper and tied with twine."

"Have you ever had a flash of memory like this before?" Ryder settled on the bed next to her, running a hand down her stiff back.

"Only once, but it was a word that came to me, not a picture."

"What was the word?"

"A name—Shelby."

The air whistled through Ryder's teeth. Julia remembered his grandmother's name and chose it for her daughter…his daughter.

"Ryder." She placed her hand on his thigh. "Why would I name my daughter after your grandmother? Why did I come here to Silverhill?"

Ryder debated just what to tell her, how honest he should be. He didn't think she was ready to hear the whole truth. "We talked a lot, Julia." He plucked her hand from his leg, turned it over, and traced a fingertip along the lines on her palm. "I told you about Silverhill, about my family's ranch and my grandmother who worked alongside my grandfather to build the ranch. Her strength and determination fascinated you."

"Because I had a life filled with frivolous parties and superficial relationships?"

"Maybe." He rubbed his thumb in the center of her hand. "But you weren't superficial. You were strong…are strong, and I think you wanted something more from your life."

"Do you think I decided to find it in Silverhill?" She folded her fingers over his thumb, capturing it against the warmth of her hand.

"I think you delivered that package to Jeremy, and something happened in Arizona, something that landed you in a stolen car with mounds of cash. You fled to Silverhill to seek the protection of my family, the family you'd heard so much about."

She shook her head and her silky brown hair slid over her shoulder. "But what? What could've happened?"

Ryder pushed up from the bed and paced in front of the window. Did he want these memories to come back for her? Would they put her in danger?

"You know." Julia jumped from the bed and blocked his

path, hands planted on her hips. "Tell me. How did Jeremy die and where?"

Ryder blew out a breath and squared his shoulders. "Jeremy was murdered over three years ago…in Arizona."

Chapter Four

A dull pain thudded against her temples and she dropped to the edge of the bed. "Three years ago in Arizona?"

"I heard about it a month after it happened." Joining her on the bed, Ryder rested an arm across her shoulders. "That's when I called you in Paris and discovered you'd left for the States."

"Arizona." She gripped the bedspread with stiff fingers. She must've seen Jeremy before he was murdered or maybe she witnessed the murder, or... "Do you think I...?"

"Had anything to do with the murder?" He stroked her hair, and his hands seemed to draw the tension out of her body. "Absolutely not. You're no expert in explosives."

"Explosives?" She jerked her head up. "Jeremy died in a bomb blast?"

"Someone planted plastiques around his house in Arizona and detonated them while Jeremy was inside. They identified his remains, or at least some jewelry he wore. The fire from the bomb blast incinerated his body."

"Do you think that's what I was running from? Do you think I was there when the house exploded and Jeremy died?"

"Maybe." Ryder plucked up one of her hands, nervously bunching the bedspread, and chafed it between his two palms.

"Julia, Jeremy was no longer working for the agency when he was killed. He was under investigation for espionage, selling State secrets."

She swallowed and the pain in her head came roaring back. Her past got crazier and crazier each time Ryder revealed a piece of information. "Did the agency kill him?"

"Black Cobra works outside the boundaries of government oversight, but not that far outside. If we gathered enough evidence, we would've arrested him and charged him with treason."

"Black Cobra? Is that the name of your agency?"

Squeezing her hand, he nodded. "Not even my family knows that, but you knew the name before. You deserve to know it now."

Black Cobra. Drawing her brows together, she grabbed Ryder's forearm and turned it around to inspect the inside, running her fingertip from his elbow to his wrist.

Ryder sucked in a sharp breath. "What is it, Julia? Do you remember something?"

"A tattoo. I remember a tattoo of a black snake, here on someone's arm."

"You remember Jeremy's tattoo." Ryder shrugged. "He had a flair for the dramatic."

She jumped up from the bed. "Oh my God, it's all going to come back to me, isn't it? With you here feeding me information, I'm going to start remembering. I'll finally know why I was in that stolen car with all the money. I'll be able to give Shelby a little bit of her father back."

Ryder stiffened, his blue eyes kindling with emotion.

"Jeremy wasn't all bad, was he, Ryder?" She dropped to her knees in front of him. "I can tell Shelby a few good things about her father, can't I?"

His jaw tightened and then he cupped her face in his hands. "Jeremy had a great sense of humor, always playing practical jokes. He attracted people to him effortlessly, could make anyone do just about anything. That's why it cut so deep when he turned."

"Why do you think he did it?" She leaned her elbows on his knees.

"He scratched and scrambled his way out of a tough neighborhood in New York. He liked money and material possessions. His government job didn't provide him with enough of either. But more than anything, Jeremy liked to take risks."

Crossing her legs, she leaned back on her hands. "I can't believe I'd fall for someone like that and actually marry him."

"You were in a vulnerable place after your father died." His lips twisted. "Jeremy swept you off your feet. He could do that to women."

"Apparently he didn't stop doing it even after we got married."

"No, but at least his infidelity opened your eyes, and you dumped him. I don't think anyone had ever dumped Jeremy before."

"I wish…" Drawing her knees to her chest, she covered her mouth with her hand. She wished Ryder with his strong presence and protective manner had been at that party in Paris instead of Jeremy. Maybe then he'd be Shelby's father instead of some unfaithful, treasonous dead man.

"Are you all right?" Ryder slid to the floor in front of her, his knees touching hers. "What do you wish, Julia?"

His intense gaze seared her face, and her mind struggled to give him what he demanded—recognition. Although her brain couldn't process Ryder McClintock, her heart could. She felt this man deep in her bones. Somehow she knew she could depend on him, had depended on him in the past. He'd saved her once, and she knew he wouldn't hesitate to do so again.

Why wouldn't he explain everything?

"You're on the floor." Shelby tumbled into the room, giggling. She wedged herself between them. "You're silly."

Plucking one of Shelby's butterscotch curls between his fingers, Ryder said, "Grown-ups like to play on the floor sometimes, too. Kids don't rule the floor."

Shelby leaned against Ryder's legs, touching a finger to his nose. "You're silly."

Her daughter knew she could depend on Ryder, too.

Ryder pushed up from the floor, tucking Shelby under one arm. "Do you ladies want to come to dinner at the McClintocks' tonight?"

Shelby squealed as Ryder swung her back and forth.

Scrambling to her feet, Julia said, "We don't want to intrude on your family. They've barely seen you since you've been home."

"You're right. They don't see me for over three years and I drop my bags at the ranch and head on out again." He set Shelby on her feet, and she reached up her arms for another ride.

"That's enough, Shelby."

"I don't mind." Ryder scooped up Shelby and carried her into the front yard. On the little patch of grass, he grasped her hands and they went around and around in a circle. Occasionally, Shelby's feet left the ground and she shrieked in excitement.

"She's a daredevil." Julia laughed and shook her head. Shelby loved to play rough, but most of the surrogate fathers she had in Silverhill favored bad backs, walked with canes or tired out after fifteen minutes of Shelby time.

After a few wobbly steps, Shelby scampered away to add to her rock collection.

"That little girl has a lot of energy." Ryder shoved his hands in the pockets of his faded jeans. "Are you sure about dinner tonight? I know Dad and Pam have heard all about our connection by now and would love to have you and Shelby over."

Julia thought about sitting around the dinner table with the McClintocks—Ryder's father, stepmother, his older brother, Rod, and various ranch hands—and shuddered. She craved peace and quiet after all the bombshells today and a night with the boisterous McClintocks promised anything but.

"I'll pass on dinner, but can you do me a favor?"

"Anything."

She blinked her eyes at the promptness of his response. He really did want to help her. "I have an appointment with my psychologist, Dr. Brody, tomorrow afternoon. Can you come with me? I think it would really help."

"I'll be there. What do you do with Shelby?"

"Millie Stoker takes her. I work with Millie's daughter, Maddy, in their antique shop most days while Millie watches Shelby." Julia knotted her hands. "I don't want to pull you away from your family."

"Don't worry about it. I'll be here for a while before my next assignment. I'll have plenty of time to catch up with the family. What time should I pick you up?"

The foliage across the road rustled and spewed out Gracie Malone and her son, Charlie. Gracie waved and made a beeline for Julia's house, Charlie in tow. "We've all heard the exciting news. Imagine, all this time the McClintocks' son knew you and you didn't even realize it. Hello, Ryder."

Ryder tipped his hat. "Gracie, Charlie. How's the B and B going?"

Gracie's rabbit-like nose twitched as her eyes darted between Julia and Ryder. "It's good. We're full up right now, but I sure wish I could find some better help. Charlie just hired a young woman, but she's a little flighty…and a little trashy. The young people who come up here to work in the summer and ski in the winter aren't very reliable, are they, Charlie?"

Charlie's mouth hung slightly ajar as he stared at Julia, and her flesh crawled where his gaze slid down her body. She could totally see him pawing through her underwear.

"Are they, Charlie?" Gracie elbowed him, and he snapped his mouth shut and shook his head. She scowled at him and then pasted a smile on her face as she turned to Ryder. "So how do you know our Julia? Have you filled her in on all the details of her past yet?"

"We're…ah…acquaintances." Ryder lifted one broad shoulder. "And we're taking it slow. Julia needs time to get her bearings and absorb everything I'm throwing at her."

Yeah, like about a million years to absorb that she had a crooked spy for an ex-husband…and she may have witnessed his murder.

RYDER PULLED his truck in front of Julia's neat little clapboard house with the white picket fence. He never thought he'd see the day when Julia Rousseau would be living behind a white picket fence…or wearing her hair in a ponytail.

Julia waved as she jogged down her front steps, hitching a large handbag over her shoulder. Ryder scrambled out of the truck to get the door for her and when she smiled her thanks, his heart flip-flopped in his chest.

His attraction to Julia hadn't been all about appearance. The sexy, sophisticated siren with the couture clothing and perfect hair and makeup hooked him from the moment he saw her, but he loved the substance beneath the glossy exterior. Jeremy never got beyond that. When Jeremy discovered his wife had a strong will and a mind of her own, the marriage crumbled. Although he didn't plan it, Ryder saw Julia through the fallout.

"How's Shelby this morning?" He glanced at Julia before cranking on the engine. "Was she upset about the break-in yesterday?"

"No. She just thought her silly mommy threw her underwear all over the bed." Julia snapped her seat belt in place.

"And how's the silly mommy?" His gaze slid sideways to her face, still tense despite the smile.

"I'm fine." She flipped the ponytail over her shoulder. "I bought some new underwear, a new bedspread and a pair of scissors. Then I had Gary the locksmith come out and reinforce all my locks."

"That's the exterior. What about the interior?" He tapped his chest with his fist.

"Of course I'm still jittery, but it's amazing what a new set of locks can do for your peace of mind." She clasped her hands between her knees. "Besides, all the stuff you told me yesterday occupied my mind more than a few sliced-up bras."

"Did you remember anything else?" He held his breath. Should he tell her about their relationship before she remembered it on her own or should he wait? She'd seemed almost relieved when she discovered Shelby's father was dead and out of the picture. Why would she want to share her daughter with a stranger?

"Nope. I've been trying to put a face and a body to that tattooed arm, but haven't had any luck." She spun around. "Do you have any pictures of Jeremy or can we get any from Black Cobra?"

"I don't have any pictures, but I may be able to get one from the agency. Do you think it will help you to remember what happened in Arizona?" He brushed his fingers down her arm. "Are you sure you want to remember?"

She shivered. "Not sure at all, but it's like bitter medicine. It'll be good for me in the end. With you giving me information and working with Dr. Brody, I think I have a shot at recovering my memories—good and bad."

"Who's this Dr. Brody? Was he the first doctor you saw?"

If so, Julia put a lot of faith in a doctor who hadn't helped her much in the past three years.

"No. Six months after the accident, I went to a hypnotist in Denver first and then a psychiatrist there. I stayed with them for six months, and they referred me to Dr. Brody in Durango, closer to home." She rubbed her palms against the thighs of her jeans. "I—it's not just to recover my memory that I see Dr. Brody."

Ryder drilled the road in front of him, gripping the steering wheel. It wasn't his place to pry. His job was to provide her with details of her past life, not ferret out the details of her new life.

She blew out a long breath. "I suffer from panic attacks."

Loosening his hold on the steering wheel, Ryder asked, "That's understandable after what you've been through. Do you take medication?"

She shook her head, the glossy ponytail skimming her shoulders. "No, I don't want to take drugs. I'd rather handle my problem through therapy and it's working. The panic attacks are decreasing. In fact, I thought about ending my sessions with Dr. Brody…until you showed up."

"Yeah, I've sent a few women into therapy."

Julia snorted. "I just bet you have."

Ryder laughed and turned up the radio for the rest of their drive into Durango. Julia bounced in her seat, singing in her off-key voice to the country music blaring from the speakers.

Some things hadn't changed at all…except maybe her choice in music.

Julia directed him to a three-story office building housing dentists and doctors, and he pulled into the underground parking structure.

Holding his breath against the exhaust fumes, Ryder followed

Julia into the elevator, asked her which floor and punched the button for the third floor. "Did you tell Dr. Brody about me?"

"I called him this morning. He's anxious to meet you. He said with my approval, you could join our session."

"I'm not sure how much help I'll be during your session, but I'll give it a try. Will Dr. Brody call on me to fill in the gaps and then question you about what you remember? Not sure how this will work."

"Didn't I tell you?" Julia grasped the door handle of Dr. Brody's office and then shoved the door open with her hip. "Dr. Brody's a hypnotist as well as a psychologist."

Ryder swallowed the lump in his throat as he entered the small office populated by Colorado landscapes. She had told him, but he thought it didn't work on her. Could this doctor coax the truth of Shelby's paternity out of Julia? Ryder wasn't ready for that yet. He wanted to get to know his daughter better, show Julia he could be a father.

Julia jabbed at a button on the wall outside another door and plopped down on a sofa in the empty office. She grabbed a magazine from the side table and thumbed through it, barely scanning the pictures of smiling celebrities.

Ryder perched on the edge of a chair across from her. Julia didn't even realize she had a nodding acquaintance with a few of those celebrities. What a strange, lonely existence she must've led these past three years.

His stomach rolled. He should've been there for her. He should've realized she was in trouble when she didn't answer his letters and disappeared after Jeremy's murder. But damn it, his job didn't allow him to pursue personal reconnaissance missions. After Jeremy sold some of Black Cobra's secrets, all the agents had to work overtime to repair the damage.

The door to the doctor's inner sanctum swung open and a

tall, dark-haired man dressed in black slacks and a white shirt leaned into the waiting room.

"Julia? Are you ready?"

"Jim." Julia tossed the magazine aside and jumped to her feet. "I'm Julia Rousseau."

In two steps, Dr. Brody landed in front of Julia and scooped her into a hug. "I'm so happy for you."

Ryder uncurled the fists clenched at his sides. Therapists had to be touchy feely to do their jobs. Even if they didn't care personally about their patients, they had to pretend to care.

Julia emerged from the embrace, wiping a tear from her cheek. "This is Ryder McClintock, the man I told you about. The man from my past."

Dr. Brody's gaze shifted to Ryder and he stuck out his hand. "Mr. McClintock, Julia told me everything on the phone this morning. I hope you can help her."

"Everything?" Ryder's pulse thumped in his throat as he glanced at Julia.

She shook her head slightly, indicating she'd withheld some of the vitals from Dr. Brody about Black Cobra.

"That's the nature of the therapeutic doctor-patient relationship, Mr. McClintock. The patient reveals everything to her doctor, and the doctor keeps those revelations in the strictest confidence."

The man's condescending tone and the little smirk that went with it made Ryder want to land a punch against the guy's jaw. Instead he ran a hand through his hair. *This isn't about you, McClintock. This is about Julia.*

"Ryder. You can call me Ryder."

"And you can call me Jim. Let's go inside my office."

Jim ushered Julia through first and she crossed the little hallway to a dimly lit office. She sank into an overstuffed chair, curling her legs beneath her, completely at home and at ease.

Ryder flexed his fingers as he took a chair in the corner. He had to tame the jealousy that surged through his veins at the intimate relationship Julia had with Dr. Brody…Jim. He'd never been to the agency shrink himself, but a few of the other agents told him about the intense connection they had with their therapists and how that connection helped with the therapeutic process.

Brody claimed the chair across from Julia, his knees almost touching hers. "I haven't used hypnosis with Julia in quite a while, but I think this is an excellent opportunity with you here, Ryder. Julia, do you agree to the hypnosis?"

"Yes." She rested her head against the cushion of the chair and closed her eyes.

Brody's soothing voice filled the space in the darkened room. "Relax your muscles, Julia. There is no tension in your body. No bones. No flesh. You are weightless."

Julia's chest rose and fell as her breathing deepened. Ryder couldn't be hypnotized. He had very little susceptibility, and then Black Cobra trained the rest out of him.

"You can no longer feel the chair beneath you, Julia. You are suspended in space. You are suspended in time. There is no continuum of time. There is only your mind and the memories buried there."

Ryder asked in a low voice, "Will she remember what she tells us under hypnosis?"

Jim nodded to Ryder and then consulted the notebook in his lap. "You're in Paris, Julia. Do you remember Paris?"

Julia murmured, *"Oui, je rappelle."*

"In English, Julia."

"I remember Paris." Julia's head fell to the side as a smile curved her lips.

"Where did you live?"

Julia described her flat in Rue St. Germains precisely how Ryder remembered it, down to the fresh flowers she kept in the blue vase on her kitchen table.

"Do you remember your husband, Jeremy Scott?"

"Yes, I remember Jeremy, but I can't see his face."

As Jim took Julia through the night she met Jeremy and their brief courtship, Ryder winced at the half smile on Julia's face. Jeremy had charmed the socks off her, along with a few other articles of clothing, while she still ached over the death of her father.

"Did you go to Arizona to see Jeremy after your divorce?"

Frowning, Julia bit her lip. "He was in Tucson. He needed something from the Paris flat—a computer disc."

Ryder's heart thudded in his chest. Had Jeremy dragged Julia into his subterfuge against Black Cobra?

Jim shot a glance at Ryder. Ryder didn't know how much Julia told him about her ex-husband's work, but like the doc said, he couldn't repeat anything outside of these four walls.

"What was on the disc, Julia?"

"I don't know, but it was bad." Her straight teeth sawed at her bottom lip. "I know it was bad, dangerous."

"Did you bring the CD to Jeremy?"

"I had to." No longer relaxed, Julia dug her fingernails into the arms of the chair. "He threatened…he said he'd expose Ryder if I didn't go to Tucson."

Ryder's head shot up. Jeremy must've known about their relationship to use that threat against Julia. Not that there was any relationship before the divorce. Ryder didn't make a habit of pursuing married women, but Julia's marriage to Jeremy disintegrated before it ever got going. Still, Jeremy wasn't the kind of man to share his toys even when he tired of them, and Jeremy definitely treated Julia like a plaything.

"Expose Ryder?" Brody tapped his pencil against his notebook in a staccato beat.

"Expose him to the enemy. Blow his cover."

Folding his arms, Ryder bunched his hands against his body to keep from reaching out to Julia. Damn. He should've been there to protect her against Jeremy and his wild demands.

"So you went to Tucson and brought the CD to Jeremy." Brody's words had a sharp edge, losing their soothing quality.

"Yes." Julia squeezed her eyes tighter, pressing the heels of her hands to her temples. "I gave him the computer disc so he wouldn't hurt Ryder."

Brody sat back in his chair and ran a hand over his mouth. "Slow down, Julia. It's all right. Ryder is safe. What happened in Tucson? What happened after you gave Jeremy the CD?"

Straightening her back, Julia unfurled her long legs and planted them on the floor. "I gave him a CD, and then he hit me. I tried to give him a different CD, a phony, but he knew."

The blood thundering in his ears, Ryder jumped up from his chair, knocking it to the floor. That SOB. Jeremy lucked out being dead.

Brody held his hand out, palm forward to stop Ryder. "Go on, Julia. What happened after Jeremy hit you?"

"A fight. An explosion." Julia drew her knees to her chest and rocked back and forth. "I don't know. I can't remember. I don't want to remember."

As her words ended on a wail, Ryder charged across the room and dropped to his knees in front of her chair. "Bring her out, doc," he shouted.

"Julia, you're here in my office. You're not in Tucson. You're safe. It's safe to come back."

She stopped rocking and collapsed back in her chair, sobbing. Whispering nonsense in her ear, Ryder gathered Julia in his arms and stroked her back. Her head fell to his shoulder as she clung to him.

She remembered. She remembered why she went to Tucson, and she remembered she'd done it to save his life. How much more would it take for her to remember their love and to figure out Shelby belonged to him?

JULIA SPLASHED cold water on her face and then gripped the edge of the vanity with wet hands as she peered into the mirror. She looked the same. Somehow she always figured when her memory returned she'd look different, she'd more closely resemble that woman who had a life and a past before Silverhill, before Shelby.

She slid the elastic band from her ponytail and shook her hair loose. Wide brown eyes stared back. Sweet, helpless, vulnerable Julia. The good people of Silverhill had treated her that way for so long, she'd become that person.

But now she knew different.

Would a sweet woman end her marriage at the first sign of infidelity?

Would a helpless woman travel halfway across the world to save her…friend?

Would a vulnerable woman escape from a murder scene and an explosion while seven months pregnant?

Why did she sleep with her ex-husband after their separation anyway? It must've been good-bye sex, and obviously Jeremy didn't know about the pregnancy until he saw her. As the memories flooded her brain during the hypnosis, she recalled that her pregnancy angered Jeremy. He hit her because of the pregnancy.

Her gut clenched and she folded her arms across her stomach. Her ex-husband was a snake, just like the one tattooed on his arm. Maybe that's why she couldn't remember his face. She could recall the anger emanating from him, but his face remained a blur.

And Ryder? Jim didn't take her down that path of memories, and despite her best efforts, she couldn't scale the wall that still existed when she thought of Ryder. She'd sensed great relief when she remembered taking the computer disc to Jeremy and knowing it would keep Ryder safe. Had they been more than good friends? The way her pulse raced in his presence indicated they'd shared something together.

She shook her head and yanked a paper towel from the dispenser. He would've told her…unless he didn't want the relationship anymore. And why would he? He remembered Julia Rousseau as a sophisticated party girl, not this broken, pathetic woman who jumped at her own shadow.

Her body jerked when someone tapped on the bathroom door.

"Julia, are you all right in there?" Ryder opened the door a crack.

"I'm fine. Give me a minute." She plowed through her purse and dug out her makeup bag. She blotted her red nose with some powder and brushed black mascara on her eyelashes. Rose lipstick completed the repairs and she shoved out of the bathroom.

Ryder and Jim, heads together, huddled outside Jim's office. Were they plotting their next assault on her mind?

They looked up with matching frowns when she cleared her throat. "Don't look so worried. I'm good. I think it was a great session. If you hadn't pulled me out, Jim, I'm sure I would've remembered precisely what happened at that bungalow in Tucson and how I wound up in that stolen car."

"You were stressing out. We'll get there." Jim leaned a shoulder against the wall.

"Good. There are other things I need to explore." Her gaze

swept to Ryder's face and then back to Jim's. "Maybe after a while I won't even need hypnosis to get there."

"That's what I'm hoping. You need some quiet time every night before you go to bed to let the memories wash over you. They'll come."

"Would you like to get something to eat while we're in Durango?" Ryder checked his watch. "Maybe dinner?"

"Sure, I'll call Millie and let her know I'll be late picking up Shelby."

"Are you sure you're all right?" Jim hugged her, pulling her body close to his for a moment, his hand hovering over her loose hair.

She stiffened. Jim had always been affectionate with her, but at times his touch felt more like a caress and occasionally his e-mails and phone calls veered more toward the personal than the professional. For a patient with no family and no past the personal touch worked, but under Ryder's watchful eye she backed out of Jim's embrace.

"I could use a drink, but I'm fine."

"And something to eat." Ryder grabbed her hand, pulling her out of Jim's sphere. "Is it okay if I leave the truck in the parking structure, Jim? There's a great steak house down the street, and we can walk from here."

Jim's gaze flicked over their clasped hands. "No problem. Julia, we'll discuss what came out of the hypnosis next week. I have one more patient for the day. Have a nice evening and try to relax. We made great progress today."

As they headed down the hallway, Ryder squeezed her hand. "You done good, kiddo."

"I didn't remember everything that happened in Tucson. I can't remember Jeremy's face and I don't know how I managed to snare a stolen car packed with cash." She screwed up her face. "I don't know why I risked giving sensitive information to Jeremy to save your life."

"You're a loyal friend." He kissed the side of her head. "But I never would've allowed you to make that trip if I'd known what you were up to."

He punched the elevator button and then cocked his head. "How do you know that CD contained sensitive information?"

"Makes sense, doesn't it? Otherwise, I could've dropped it in the mail. No, Jeremy wanted me to hand-deliver that disc."

The elevator rumbled down to the lobby of the building and placing his hand against the small of her back, Ryder steered Julia toward the front door. "Let's give your brain a break and satisfy some of those primal needs."

Julia dropped her lashes and shot a glance at Ryder from beneath them. It had been a while since she'd thought about her primal needs, but Ryder McClintock had all the equipment to satisfy them.

After a heavy meal of steak and potatoes, Julia leaned her head back against the leather banquette. "I feel like I've been talking about me and Shelby all through dinner. What about you? Why'd you leave this beautiful place for a life of secrets in foreign places?"

"You've met the McClintock bunch. Isn't it obvious?"

She swirled her ruby-colored merlot, which Ryder knew to order for her without even asking. "Your stepmother's a control freak, your father's autocratic, your older brother, Rod, seems to be following in his boot steps, and your younger brother, Rafe, came back to Silverhill after working as a cop in L.A. just to prove to them that he had his own sphere of authority."

Ryder grinned and tossed his napkin on the table. "You just about nailed that. Now you know why I left."

"To prove yourself, but you took an extreme route."

"I didn't need to prove myself." He twisted the napkin. "I just don't like being ordered around like some clueless ranch hand."

Did she lose her social skills along with her memory? She had no right to poke and prod at Ryder. Her fingers danced along the grooves between his knuckles. "I'm sorry. I didn't mean to judge you. I just know that with two larger-than-life figures like Ralph and Rod McClintock looming over my shoulder, I'd feel like I had to prove something."

The grin returned and his fist flattened out beneath her hand. "Touchy subject, but then you never did mince words. Are you sure you don't want dessert?"

"I'm good. I'm anxious to get home to Shelby."

"I don't blame you."

"D-do you have children? Here I'm assuming you're not married."

Ryder slid out of the booth and turned to get his hat from the rack on the side of the booth. "I've never been married and I don't have kids."

She caught the sigh of relief before it escaped from her lips. Although Ryder's unmarried state pleased her, she'd never seen a bachelor handle a little girl like Ryder handled Shelby. He'd make a great dad someday.

They left the restaurant and strolled along the sidewalk back to the medical building that housed Dr. Brody's office.

"I hope Dr. Brody was right and it was okay to leave the truck in the parking lot." Ryder quickened his pace as they drew closer to the parking garage.

"It should be fine."

Forgoing the elevator, they climbed the steps to the second floor of the parking structure and banged through the metal door. Just a few cars remained in spaces on the far end of the lot, Ryder's truck among them.

"What the hell?" Ryder stiffened beside her and then covered the distance to his truck with his long stride while she hurried behind him.

"What's wrong?"

"My tire's flat." Ryder crouched behind the truck and swore. "Both of my back tires are flat."

A spiral of fear zinged up Julia's spine as her gaze darted between the two tires. Both of them had ragged gashes along the inside and outside. "Ryder, someone slashed your tires."

He pushed off the bumper and circled to the front of the truck. "They did a number on the front tires too and smeared my windshield."

Julia leaned around him to peer at the windshield and then clutched her stomach. Someone didn't just smear the windshield. Someone had left a message: *Leave or die.*

Chapter Five

Julia swayed against Ryder, and he caught her. "What's wrong?"

Then he saw the words on his windshield and hot anger thudded in his veins. Did Julia's stalker follow them here? Was this some kind of warning for him?

"It's him, isn't it?"

She spoke the words against his chest, and he felt her warm breath through his shirt. He held her close, his gaze tracking through the parking garage. The coward hit and then ran.

"This message is for you, Ryder." A tremble rolled through her body. "He must've seen us together. He's going to come after you now."

"I hope he does." He smoothed his hands down her back, soothing away the ripples of fear. "Because he owes me a new set of tires. Underwear, tires, this guy's going to rack up a big bill by the time he's through with his juvenile games."

"Do you think that's all it is?"

Maybe yes, maybe no, but he didn't want to frighten Julia any further. She'd been through enough today with memories of Jeremy's death galloping through her head.

Ryder didn't fear for his own safety, but if this guy was crazy enough to follow them to Durango, slash a set of expensive tires and write a warning on his windshield, he posed a grave threat to Julia. And possibly to Shelby.

"We'll let the cops figure it out." He slid his cell phone out of his pocket and called the Durango Sheriff's Department. They'd have to tell the cops back home about this incident. He wished his brother, Rafe, would hurry up and get out of the academy. He'd feel a helluva lot better with Rafe on this case than Zack Ballard.

A deputy from the Durango Sheriff's Department showed up, dusted for prints and shrugged it off as malicious vandalism. Even when they told him about the break-in at Julia's house, he lifted a shoulder and snapped his notebook shut. "Nothing much I can do about that here, folks. Even if the sheriffs in Silverhill get a print from your house, we got nothing here."

Ryder called a tow truck and he and Julia stood outside the tire shop, which accepted the truck and then closed for the night.

"Taxi?" Ryder scuffed the toe of his boot on the sidewalk.

"That would cost a fortune. Too bad the Silverhill-Durango Railroad doesn't run on weeknights."

"Rental car? I think my insurance will cover that."

Julia brushed a wisp of hair from her eyes, her shoulders sagging for a brief moment before she forced her lips into a smile. "Sure. I guess we can call information on my cell phone for the nearest rental car place. I didn't see any on the way to and from dinner, but then I wasn't looking."

Ryder shoved his hand in his pocket, his gaze tracking over Julia's disheveled hair and the dark smudge on her chin where she'd touched her face after running her fingers along one mangled tire. They'd have to find a rental car company, make the long drive back, and then Julia would pick up Shelby from the Stokers and get her to bed. He had no doubt she'd manage it all, but why should she have to?

Clasping her shoulders, he said, "Why don't we just find a place for tonight? The tires will be ready tomorrow morning, and Shelby can stay with Clem and Millie."

"I—I think I'd like that. I'm exhausted."

"Will Shelby be okay? Seems like the Stokers treat her like an adopted granddaughter."

"They do. You know I took their last name. We've been Julia and Shelby Stoker for over three years now." Her bottom lip quivered.

His gut clenched. She should be Shelby McClintock, just like his grandmother. He expelled a breath and ran the pad of his thumb across the dirt on Julia's chin. "Shelby will be okay."

Smiling, Julia blinked her eyes. "Of course she will. The Stokers' granddaughter, Meg, is visiting for a few weeks, so the girls can have a sleepover."

She scooped her cell phone out of her purse and explained to the Stokers about Ryder's flat tires. He noticed she didn't mention the warning on the windshield.

"It's all set." She snapped her cell phone shut. "Shelby's thrilled to have a sleepover with Meg." She waved the phone. "Do we need this to find a hotel?"

"Nope, I saw one near the restaurant. Nothing fancy, but it'll do." He gripped her elbow and propelled her down the sidewalk.

"Good, if it's near the restaurant, we can stop in at the pharmacy in Dr. Brody's office building to pick up a few essentials, at least some toothpaste and a couple of toothbrushes."

When they got to the pharmacy, they wandered through the shelves picking up toothpaste, toothbrushes, dental floss and a comb. While Julia thumbed through a magazine, Ryder hesitated in front of the rack of condoms.

Was he insane? Julia wasn't ready for that. Maybe she never would be.

She dropped the magazine and spun around, her gaze flicking to the shelf in front of him. "Are you ready?"

With heat rising from his chest, he spun around and grabbed a bag of chocolate-covered peanuts. "Just picking up a few snacks in case they have a movie channel."

Raising her brows, she snapped up a bag of jelly beans. "Just gotta make sure we use that floss."

They paid for their odd assortment of items and Ryder swung the door open for Julia, nearly colliding with Dr. Brody barreling through the door. Ryder dropped the plastic bag, and a toothbrush spilled onto the ground.

"Sorry about that." Brody stooped over and plucked the toothbrush from the ground. His eyes narrowed as he handed it back to Ryder. His hand trembled slightly. "What are you two still doing here?"

"Long story." Ryder snatched the brush and dropped it back in the bag. "My tires were slashed."

"In the parking garage?" Brody ran a hand through his hair, his eyes widening behind his glasses.

"Yeah, right where we left the truck after our appointment with you."

"Did you call the police? We've had a few break-ins in that garage. We may need to hire some security." His gaze darted between the bag in Ryder's hand and the one dangling from Julia's wrist.

"We called the Sheriff's Department. No evidence or prints. I'm getting new tires tomorrow morning, but for now…"

"For now I'm just too tired to face the drive home, so we're staying here tonight." Julia swung the bag from her fingertips. "Toothbrushes and all. What about you? I thought you had one last patient after us."

Brody brushed past them. "The patients leave, but the

work doesn't stop. Have a nice evening, and I'll see you both next week."

When they got outside, Ryder took the bag from Julia. "Did Dr. Brody seem upset to you?"

"Maybe a little agitated. Perhaps he had a rough session. Mine was no piece of cake, either."

"Stop dancing around, Julia. Dr. Jim Brody is attracted to you."

"I don't know." She tilted her head but didn't sound surprised. "It may just be that intimate therapeutic thing. It's called transference."

Ryder snorted. "Transference is when the patient falls for the doctor, not the other way around. I think that's called countertransference or an ethics violation."

They stopped before the hotel's entrance and Julia placed a hand on one hip. "What are you implying, Ryder? Do you think Jim is responsible for cutting your tires and the message on the windshield?"

"I don't know, Julia. I'm just wondering how eager Dr. Jim is for you to recover your memories and have no more use for him or his services."

A LITTLE TWIST of disappointment niggled her belly when Ryder booked two adjoining rooms. What did she expect, the honeymoon suite with a heart-shaped bed and a mirror on the ceiling? Although she had caught him eyeing the condoms.

As Ryder explained their predicament to the hotel clerk, the clerk just nodded with one cocked eyebrow. Probably assumed they were married to other people and having a torrid affair.

Julia gripped the handle of the plastic bags from the pharmacy. Why did that thought spring into her head? Would she have done something like that when she was married to Jeremy? Is that why their marriage ended? If Ryder played the part of the "other man," he probably wouldn't be too eager to fess up to it.

She knew she and Ryder shared a connection in her past. She could feel it down to the tips of her toes, which had a habit of curling every time Ryder touched her. And what about Shelby…?

Ryder smacked the pen on the counter and swept the card key into his palm. "That should do it. We're on the second floor."

Following him upstairs, Julia wrinkled her nose at the musty smell from the carpet. Not exactly the type of place she'd want to have a secret assignation. She tugged on Ryder's sleeve. "I hope the rooms are clean."

"I think the place is old, not dirty. We can hop in a taxi and find someplace else if you want."

"This is fine. There's no guarantee another hotel will have any rooms available anyway, and I can't face wandering around Durango looking for a place to stay. It's just for one night." Truthfully, the discoveries she made in Dr. Jim's office and the slashed tires had taken their toll. She just wanted to sit and vegetate.

Ryder slid the card in the lock and ushered her inside. The small room held a queen-size bed with two nightstands, a bureau with a TV built in on the top and a desk and chair by the window. The bathroom had a fresh-scrubbed, antiseptic smell.

Ryder pushed open the door to the adjoining room, which had an identical setup with a blue color scheme instead of green. "Which one do you want?"

"I'll take the blue room."

He left the door ajar and gestured to the TV. "Want to join me for a movie?" He turned on the TV and clicked through the stations. "Aha, movie channel. Did you see that comedy from last summer? I heard it's funny. I missed everything where I was, so it's brand new to me."

"Where were you?" She dropped to the edge of the bed and toed off her flats.

He pulled off his boots, plumped several pillows against the headboard and reclined on the bed, facing the TV. "Can't tell you that."

She sighed and wriggled back on the bed. "If Jeremy was anything like you, I probably didn't have much to forget anyway." She paused. "Was Jeremy anything like you?"

"Naw." He grinned. "I'm a big, dumb cowboy from Colorado. Jeremy was a slick, sophisticated New Yorker with charm to spare."

Julia rolled on her side, digging her elbow into the soft mattress and propping up her head. If Jeremy had more charm than Ryder, he must've been oozing it. "I thought he came from a poor family. Where'd he get the sophistication?"

"He studied it and then perfected it."

"Is that why I fell for him, his charm?"

"Pretty much." Ryder grabbed one of the bags from the night-stand, pulled out the jelly beans and ripped open the bag. "Like I said, you were in a rough place. Your father died less than a year before you met Jeremy. He charmed you, made you laugh, made you want to take hold of life with both hands again."

"Then he betrayed me...and you."

"Don't beat yourself up, Julia. We were all taken in by Jeremy, even the agency." He held out a handful of jelly beans after picking out all the black ones. "You don't like the black ones."

He poured the jelly beans into her palm, and she pinched a purple one between her fingers. "Who killed Jeremy and why? And whoever it was, do you think they got the disc I brought to Jeremy?"

"Probably a foreign agency murdered him. Maybe the same agency he planned to sell the disc to. Maybe they didn't want to pay him. Maybe they smelled a double cross. A million things could've happened. Even if Brody didn't bring you out of your trance when he did, you may not have the answer."

"Did anything happen after Jeremy's murder? Was any information compromised?"

"Not that we know of. The movie's starting. Do you want to watch it or continue poking around your brain?"

She shook her head and popped the jelly bean into her mouth, biting into the sweet grape flavor. "My brain's done for the night."

"Then get up here and get comfortable." He punched a stack of pillows beside him on the bed.

She crawled up next to him and wedged her back against the headboard. "This better be funny because I'm ready to laugh."

Giggling and snorting at the juvenile antics of the characters on the small screen with her thigh pressed firmly against Ryder's, Julia experienced a comfort in her own skin that she usually felt only when holding Shelby in her arms.

When the movie ended, she didn't want to retreat to her own room and a cold bed. "Do you want to watch the historical drama that's on next?"

"Sure, do any heads roll in this one? I only watch historical dramas with lots of blood and gore."

"It's the French Revolution. I'm sure heads are going to roll."

"I'm in."

"I'm going to brush my teeth first." She rolled off the bed and padded into the bathroom where they put the toothbrushes and floss. How long could she stall and make this moment last with Ryder?

When she returned to the room, Ryder had scrunched down farther on the bed, his long legs crossed at the ankles and his feet nearly reaching the foot of the mattress.

"Any blood yet?" She bounced next to him on the bed.

"Not yet, but it's looking pretty good."

She snuggled next to him, her cheek brushing his shoulder. If he took her in his arms right now, if he kissed her...well, she wouldn't be responsible for her actions.

Instead he rubbed the top of her foot with his, and her toes curled again. If she couldn't have the kiss, this was almost as good.

Warm, safe, secure. She remembered these feelings with this man. When would Ryder McClintock finally tell her what they had meant to each other in her past life? Maybe if she had a spine like the old Julia, she'd ask him.

SHE GRIPPED the handle of the car door and tugged at it, peering over her left shoulder at the man charging out the front door of the house.

"Julia!"

The explosion ripped through the little stucco house, a ball of orange flames ringed in black smoke huffing out to encompass the angry man shouting her name.

Now screaming her name.

"Julia!"

Her cheekbone throbbed where he'd punched her, and the heat from the inferno scorched her back. She had to get away. She had to protect her baby.

"Julia!"

The fire alarm cut through the smoke and flames, an insistent blaring sound that mixed with the man yelling her name.

"Julia!"

She jerked awake to find herself in a sitting position, clasped in Ryder's arms.

"Julia, wake up."

Her nostrils flared at the acrid smell of smoke and she thrashed her legs, kicking Ryder's shin.

"We have to get out." Ryder pushed up from the bed, his arm wrapped around her waist. He stuffed her shoes inside his boots and yanked them from the floor with one hand. "Let's go."

He half dragged her out of the room, while she rubbed her eyes. "What is it? What's happening?"

Ryder grabbed her hand and pulled her down the staircase leading to the lobby.

"The hotel's on fire."

Chapter Six

Julia hugged her denim jacket to her chest. The daytime temperatures reached a comfortable seventy-two degrees today, but the nights dropped to the forties…and she hadn't planned on being outside during the night.

The red lights from the fire engines played across the hotel guests' shocked faces. People in various stages of undress scattered along the sidewalk across the street from the hotel, which had black smoke billowing out of one side.

The side where she and Ryder had their rooms.

Ryder snaked an arm around her shoulders, and she leaned into him for warmth. She said, "I'm glad you woke up. I was sound asleep. I didn't even hear the fire alarm."

She covered her mouth. She did hear the fire alarm, but she'd incorporated it into her dream. The dream of a small house exploding and a man rushing out of that house to drag her back inside. Jeremy. She couldn't see his face in the dream, either. Under hypnosis she'd recalled a fight. Was that fight between her and Jeremy? She shivered, but not from the cold this time.

"Are you all right?" Ryder squeezed her closer. "Are you thinking what I'm thinking?"

Since Ryder couldn't be thinking about her dream, she shook her head. "What do you mean?"

"That we'll have to find another place to sleep tonight." He patted the back pocket of his jeans. "At least I had time to grab my wallet and ID."

Clutching Ryder's arm, she coughed at the smoky air filling her lungs. "That's not what you meant. You think someone set this fire on purpose. The same someone who slashed your tires."

"The thought crossed my mind when I heard one of the firemen mention arson. The fire started in the laundry room, which was beneath our room. Dr. Brody knew we were spending the night. Maybe he followed us here."

"That's crazy." She shrugged out of the arm encircling her. "Jim might have a small crush on me, but he's not a lunatic."

"Julia, psychologists are not supposed to have crushes on their patients, small or otherwise. How come the guy hasn't been able to help you recover one memory in over three years? Think about it."

"Do you think he's running over to Silverhill to leave me flowers and paw through my underwear, too?"

"Maybe."

"Okay, that's enough. No more talk about Jim being a crazed stalker. I'm cold, I'm tired and I want to go home." She clenched her jaw to stop the flow of childish complaints. Ryder had suffered as much as she.

And she hadn't wanted to go home as long as she'd snuggled next to him on the bed scarfing up jelly beans and laughing at silly pratfalls. She hadn't wanted to move one inch until this latest catastrophe.

Did her secret admirer plan to pull her and Ryder apart with this fire? She hugged herself. Secret admirers didn't slash tires or set fires. His actions today catapulted him from secret admirer to scary stalker. How much farther would he go?

"I'm sorry." Ryder took her hand, lacing his fingers through hers. "I'm not here to try and convict Brody, and the fire could be a coincidence. Let's check in with the desk clerk. He's on his cell phone finding rooms for all the guests."

Julia stood close to Ryder as the clerk made arrangements to book them into two rooms a mile away. She surveyed the people on the sidewalk, faces distorted by the revolving red and blue lights, gathered to watch the firemen extinguish the last of the flames.

Was one of them responsible for the fire? Did the crowd conceal her stalker? She curled her fingers around Ryder's belt loop as a scary thought flashed through her mind, giving her goose bumps.

What if she didn't even know her stalker?

What if he was a stranger?

"I GOT SOMETHING for you on Dr. James Brody."

Ryder gripped the cell phone, his pulse quickening. "Hold on just a minute, Wade."

The din of his father and older brother, Rod, arguing in the kitchen assaulted his ears, and his stepmother's voice on the phone arguing with a member of her charitable committee made him cringe. So much for a relaxing leave in the bosom of his family.

Ryder pushed up from the sofa and headed outside so he could hear what Wade Parker, his FBI buddy, had to say about Dr. Jim Brody.

He leaned against the front porch railing, hitching his boot up on the ledge. "Whaddya got? Does he have a record?"

"No, he has a censure."

"What the hell does that mean?"

"The American Board of Professional Psychologists censured Dr. Brody for exhibiting inappropriate behavior with a patient."

"What did he do?" Ryder clenched his jaw. If Brody turned out to be Julia's tormenter, he'd personally make sure he couldn't practice his "talking profession" for a long time.

"He allowed a patient to spend the night at his house when she left her husband."

Ryder exhaled. Brody may be unethical, but that didn't mean he sliced up women's panties for kicks. "Did he advise his patient to leave her husband? No conflict of interest there."

"I don't know anything else, man. Those psychologists have a lot of rules governing them, and Brody broke this particular rule. I don't know if he went on to have a relationship with this woman or not."

"Okay, I appreciate it, Wade."

"I can tell by your voice you expected deeper, darker deeds from this guy, but that's all he's got on his record. Is he someone we need to watch?"

No, Brody was someone *he* needed to watch. "I was just curious. He's my…friend's therapist and seems a little too invested in her welfare."

Ryder ended the call and drilled the mountain landscape with his gaze. Could it be that simple? One overly enthusiastic psychologist with a loose grasp on ethical conduct? It sure as hell didn't feel simple to Julia, but the alternatives sucked the air out of his lungs.

Who murdered Jeremy and did the killer know Julia witnessed it? Maybe her amnesia saved her life. Would regaining her memory endanger it?

He glanced at his watch. He'd invited Julia and Shelby to

the ranch to give Shelby a riding lesson. Ever since the incidents in Durango two days ago, he'd set himself up as Julia's protector. She didn't seem to mind. She used their time together to pepper him with questions about her past, and he filled her in…up to a point.

He didn't want to spring Shelby's paternity on Julia just yet. She needed time. Oh hell, he needed time. Was he ready to be a father? Was Julia ready to give Shelby a father? She'd admitted to him that she felt a guilty relief at the news that she was a widow. She didn't want to share Shelby with a stranger.

By the time he told Julia they had a daughter together, he wouldn't be a stranger anymore. He'd make sure of that.

A car's engine buzzed in the distance, and he saw the cloud of dirt rise at the end of the drive before he spotted Julia's little silver car.

She pulled up behind his truck with the four new tires and hopped out, waving. She opened the back door of her car, and Shelby scrambled out of her car seat. Shelby's small legs churned, propelling her up the wooden steps of the porch.

"Am I going to ride a pony?" She tugged at his hand while she planted one foot on his boot.

He lifted her high and shook her back and forth. "You sure are, and I know just the pony."

"Silverbell." The screen door banged behind him, and his father stepped onto the porch. Dad chucked Shelby under the chin. "Hey there, little lady. Ready for your first riding lesson?"

"Skipper." The screen door banged again, and Rod joined them on the porch, folding his arms across his chest. "Skipper's a better choice for Shelby. She's only what, four years old?"

Ryder rolled his eyes at Julia, leaning against her car grinning. His father and Rod would argue about the color of the sky.

"Three and a half." Shelby snatched the hat from Ryder's head.

"Hell, boy." Dad punched Rod on the shoulder. "Silverbell might be a little frisky, but Shelby can handle him. She's named after my mother, isn't she?"

Rod's blue eyes narrowed as his gaze shifted between Ryder and Shelby. "Yeah, she is."

Ryder turned his back on his know-it-all older brother and jogged down the steps. "Let's get one of those ponies saddled up."

JULIA SANK onto the porch swing in front of the McClintocks' ranch house. Her anxiety about Shelby's first riding lesson had seeped away as she watched Ryder, one hand firmly on Skipper's rein, the other on Shelby's back, circle the paddock with the pony.

Shelby had accompanied Ryder to the barn to watch him rub down the horse and feed him an apple, and Julia had let her go without a backward glance. Just a week ago, she'd rarely let Shelby out of her sight, except for her stays with the Stokers.

She instinctively trusted Ryder deep in her core.

The screen door squeaked on its hinges, and Julia jerked her head to the side. Rod McClintock, Ryder's older brother, sauntered onto the porch and settled his shoulders against a post, a toothpick between his teeth.

The first time she'd seen Rod, her heart jumped in her chest. And now she knew why. Ryder resembled his older brother. They had the same strong, handsome face with wide cheekbones and a square jaw. Rod was a little taller than Ryder, a little broader, and much more serious.

His icy blue eyes drilled her, and she suppressed a shiver. He had a reputation as a hard man to please. Many women in Silverhill and beyond had tried, and many had failed.

He shifted his toothpick to the side of his mouth. "Is Ryder still with Shelby?"

"He took her to the barn to rub down Skipper." She released her toe from the porch, nudging the swing into motion.

"I never knew Ryder to be interested in kids before."

"He worked with Shelby's father, and he was…is my friend." She curled one leg beneath her thigh and continued swinging. "He told you how we knew each other, didn't he?"

"Yeah, I heard the story."

Ryder wouldn't have told his brother about Jeremy's murder and the CD. Ryder didn't tell his family a lot about what he did. Rod seemed to have his suspicions, but Julia wasn't about to fill him in.

"Well, I think Ryder feels responsible for me and Shelby, and he's helping me recover my memories."

"How's that going for you?" The lines in Rod's face softened and his voice warmed.

Julia let out a long breath. Guess he was done with the inquisition. "It's going great. With Ryder's help I'm beginning to remember things about my mom. I may even be ready to write her a letter soon and let her know she has a granddaughter."

"Let who know she has a granddaughter?" Ryder had come around the corner and balanced one foot on the bottom porch step.

"My mother."

Rod leaned his back against the porch railing and shifted the toothpick to the other side of his mouth while his gaze meandered between Julia and Ryder. Julia's cheeks warmed under his scrutiny. Unlike a lot of the good people of Silverhill, Rod had never paid much attention to her and her strange story but his brother's involvement seemed to pique his interest.

Ryder laughed. "Better go slow with that news. You don't want to turn Celeste's hair gray overnight with the shock."

"Where's Shelby?" It showed how much she'd come to trust

Ryder in such a short space of time that she didn't jump out of her skin with worry when he didn't show up with her daughter.

Ryder jerked his thumb over his shoulder. "I dropped her off at the side door of the kitchen so Pam could feed her. Is that okay?"

She nodded, and Rod snorted.

Ryder's brow shot up. "Commentary?"

"Pam must've been in heaven getting that little girl in her kitchen." Rod shoved off the porch railing and headed back inside the house. He twisted his head over his shoulder and murmured, "She's been waiting a long time for a grandkid."

"Shelby did great today." Ryder sprang up the remaining steps and dropped to the swing next to Julia, sending it rocking back and forth. "She's a natural. I don't think she has an ounce of fear in her, and Rod nailed it, as usual, Skipper was a perfect mount."

"Whoa." Julia placed a hand on Ryder's bicep and squeezed. "Slow down. You sound as excited as Shelby."

"She has that effect on me." He placed his hand over hers, rubbing the rough pad of his thumb across her knuckles. "I didn't get a chance to ask you earlier if any more memories are filtering through."

"Little by little I'm remembering events like snapshots. I— I remember my father." She placed a palm on her chest as a fist squeezed her heart.

At the end of every day, she lay on her bed and used the relaxation techniques Dr. Brody taught her. For the first time in three years, the techniques worked. Memories like wisps of gossamer thread floated through her mind. She tried to catch the happy ones and wrap them around her fingers, but she seemed to get all tangled up in the unhappy ones instead and they flooded her reeling senses with grief and loss.

Maybe her brain shoveled out the bad memories before the good ones as a kind of protective mechanism, as in, it can only get better from here. If so, this process meant good news about Ryder because try as she might, she couldn't focus on one memory of him although she felt his presence in the background.

She called Jim every day to report on her progress, and he told her the memories of Ryder might be slower to come because he existed for her in the present.

"Are you there now?"

"What?" She dropped her hands to her lap.

"Are you remembering your father now?" He draped his arm across the back of the swing, his fingertips brushing her shoulder.

"No, I'm thinking about Dr. Brody."

Ryder withdrew his arm and stiffened beside her. Damn. She'd only been thinking about Jim and his comments about Ryder. Could she backtrack now?

"I mean I'm thinking about Dr. Brody's assessment of my memories…." She trailed off as Ryder's frown deepened.

"About Brody."

She waited, but Ryder suddenly found his fingernail immensely interesting.

"Yeah, what about him?" She tried to nudge the swing into motion again, but Ryder's feet planted on the porch prevented that.

"Julia, I don't think Dr. Brody is the best therapist for you."

"You don't still think he had anything to do with slashing your tires or the fire at the hotel, do you?"

"I don't know. It's just that…" He rubbed his palms on the thighs of his jeans. "Oh hell, I had him checked out."

"You had Jim investigated?" She jumped up from the swing and dug her fists into her hips. Just because this man knew her from her past, helped her recover her memories and sent her pulse racing every time he touched her, didn't give him the right to stick his nose in her personal business.

"Do you want to know what my guy discovered?" He plucked

his white cowboy hat from his head, dropped it on the cushion she just vacated, and ran his long fingers through his hair.

She swallowed and nodded.

"The American Board of Professional Psychologists filed a formal complaint against Dr. Brody for inappropriate conduct with a patient four years ago."

"And?" Her chest ached with pent-up breath. "Did he leave her flowers, rip up her underwear and slash her tires?"

"No." He pushed up from the porch swing and it rocked back, banging the back of his legs as it swung forward. "He allowed her to spend the night at his place when she separated from her husband. I don't know anything more than that. The complaint doesn't give specifics."

Her knees felt weak with relief and she leaned against the porch railing, wedging her elbows on the top railing. "So you don't know what happened when she spent the night there? He could have just been giving her refuge. Maybe the husband was abusive."

"Why does that matter? If it's inappropriate conduct, it's inappropriate conduct. At the very least, it shows a lack of judgment."

A flash of heat claimed Julia's cheeks as she recalled a few of Jim's personal e-mails and phone calls to her. Ryder was right. Jim broke the rules, but that didn't make him a bad therapist...or a dangerous one.

"I'm supposed to fire someone I've been seeing for three years because of one mistake or just because you tell me to?"

"Like I told you before, Julia, maybe Brody hasn't been much help to you because he doesn't want you to recover your memory. If he has a thing for you, he wants to keep you dependent on him."

She narrowed her eyes. "Seems to be a lot of that going around."

Ryder gripped her shoulders and shook her. "He has a

history. Even if he's not slashing panties and tires, he's not the best choice for a therapist—not for you."

Ryder made sense. Jim belonged to that twilight life she'd been living for the past three years as a frightened, uncertain woman jumping at shadows and bumps in the night. She knew from Ryder's descriptions and her own memories, she really didn't have anything in common with that woman anymore… except Shelby.

"Maybe…" Her cell phone chirped in her purse and she held up her hand to Ryder as she shrugged out of his grasp. She snagged her purse from the porch by the side of the swing and dug out her phone. "Hello?"

"Julia, this is Sheriff Ballard."

"Hi, Sheriff." Ryder spun around and she raised her brows at him. "Did you discover anything about the break-in at my house?"

"No, it's not that. I got a call this morning from Craig Settles. Do you remember him?"

"Yes." She clutched the phone and licked her lips. "He's the owner of the stolen car I was driving when I crashed."

Ryder planted himself in front of her, mouthing words she couldn't understand.

"Right. He was cleaning his garage and discovered that old duffel bag the police recovered from the car. He found something in there he didn't notice when he first got his stuff back."

"What is it?" Her dry mouth could barely form the words. If she hid something in that car, it couldn't be good.

"A computer disc."

The blood pounded in her ears and she gripped the chain of the porch swing for support. Ryder's hand curled around her waist as he urged her to sit down.

"How does he know, how can he remember whether or not it belongs to him after all this time?"

"There's writing on the case he doesn't recognize, and he popped it in his computer and got some gibberish about encryption. He can't even read what's on it."

She and Ryder hadn't told Sheriff Ballard about the CD she delivered to Jeremy in Arizona. It looked as though she never delivered the real one after all. Was that why she and Jeremy were fighting before the house blew up? "Is Settles going to send it?"

"He already did. I'm holding it in my hand right now. He called to tell me to expect it today, but it arrived yesterday."

"Have you tried it in your computer?"

"I get the same thing—gibberish. The way I see it, this CD probably belongs to you or whoever stole the car in the first place. Do you want it?"

She didn't want anything to do with the CD. Jeremy had used it to threaten Ryder and it may have gotten Jeremy killed instead. The CD signaled trouble, but it might be important for Ryder.

She expelled a long breath. "Yeah, I want it."

"Are you at home? I can drop it off or if I can raise Zack on the radio, I'll have him come in and take it to you."

"I'm at the McClintocks' ranch, but I can be home in half an hour."

Dropping onto the swing, Julia ended the call and held her phone cupped in her palm.

Ryder whistled. "Let me guess, the owner of the stolen car found a computer disc that didn't belong to him. Wasn't that car totaled?"

Drawing her leg up, Julia balanced her chin on her knee. "I totaled the car, but the cops salvaged a duffel bag out of the trunk, along with the bag of money in the backseat. The duffel bag had a few tools in it and some fishing gear. They figured it didn't belong to me. When they contacted Craig Settles about the car, he claimed the duffel bag. I guess nobody searched it thoroughly…until now."

A chill rippled up her spine and she hunched her shoulders.

Ryder's strong hands massaged her neck, and she wished she could just collapse like a rag doll into his arms, let him handle everything. She wanted her memories to stop right here. She didn't need to know anything more about her dangerous ex-husband or his lies and deceit.

The touch of Ryder's hands melted the tension in her back, flooded her with warmth, filled her with strength. She straightened her shoulders and pushed up out of the swing. "I'm going to meet Sheriff Ballard at my house to get that CD."

"You're not going alone. If Ballard can't read that CD, neither can you, but the agency just might have a chance. You're not keeping that CD in your possession for more than thirty seconds."

Fingers of uneasiness trailed across her flesh. She didn't want the damn thing. She'd turn it over to Ryder and his spook buddies to decipher.

Ryder's stepmother, Pam, stepped out onto the porch, planting her hands on a pair of slim hips. "Are you leaving, Julia? Shelby's napping. That little girl was born to ride. Can't tell you how nice it is to have another female in the house."

Pam, like her husband, was larger than life, tall and wiry and tough as shoe leather. She and Ralph had been married for almost twenty years and rumor had it that she'd been having an affair with Ralph while he was still married to Ryder's mother. When Ralph and his wife divorced, Pam went from part-time ski instructor to reigning queen of Silverhill.

Pam's affection for Shelby surprised Julia. Rod said she'd been waiting for a grandchild, but Julia figured Pam would prefer a boy to a girl. She probably got a kick out of Shelby's tomboy tendencies.

"Why don't we let Shelby nap here until we get that…other business settled." Ryder put on his hat and tipped it over his forehead to hide his face.

"Is that all right with you, Pam?"

"That's fine with me as long as you don't mind coming all the way back out here to pick her up."

"I'll get her for Julia."

"Really?" Pam raised a brow that disappeared beneath the fluff of blond hair on her forehead. "You're taking your responsibility toward Julia seriously, aren't you? It's good to see you care for something or someone close to home." Pam turned to Julia and smirked. "That's my three boys. Ryder feels responsible for the whole world, not so much his family. Rod feels responsible for this ranch and Rafe feels responsible only for himself."

"We better get out of here." Scowling, Ryder grabbed Julia's hand. "Don't get Pam started on the defects of me and Rafe."

Pam waved from the porch. "Take your time."

"Does Pam really think protecting the country and protecting and serving as a cop are defects?"

"I don't know what her problem is. She should be down on her hands and knees thanking me every day. I'm the one who spilled the beans to my mother about the affair between my father and Pam, which led to my parents' divorce and left the field wide open for Pam."

"You? Your father and Pam have been married for quite a while. You couldn't have been more than…"

"Ten." His lips tightened. "I was ten years old and I'd been up at Snowhill skiing with my friends. I saw my father with Pam, but they didn't see me. Later that night during dinner, I asked him in front of the entire family what he and the blond ski instructor were doing up at Snowhill Lodge."

Julia caught her breath. Ryder blamed himself for his parents' divorce? "What happened?"

"My parents excused all of us from the room and proceeded to have a huge fight. Apparently, it wasn't the first time my father had checked out the ski instructors. My mother left the next day and never came back."

"You mean you never saw your mother after that? Even now?"

"That's right." Ryder squinted into the sun and reached for his sunglasses on the truck's console, squeezing them so tightly, they looked ready to snap.

"That's not your fault, Ryder."

"Oh no?" He lifted a shoulder. "Doesn't matter now. You'd think I'd be Pam's favorite stepson, but Rod is the golden boy for staying at the ranch. The McClintock Ranch means more to Pam than most of the McClintocks."

Julia wanted to erase the tightness from Ryder's face, ease the pain edging his voice. "Yeah, I'm afraid I disappointed my mother by becoming a tour guide instead of going into fashion design." She clapped a hand over her mouth.

Ryder jerked his head around. "You remember that, huh?"

"It just came to me, the feeling, the emotion, everything." She pressed her hands to her belly to still the butterfly wings.

"I suppose that's going to start happening more frequently now." Ryder gripped the steering wheel and drilled the road ahead with narrowed eyes.

"If it does, I have you to thank."

"Yeah, you have me to thank."

Ryder seemed lost in his own thoughts, so for the rest of the ride home Julia stared out the window as snatches of scenery flew by. Every once in a while, her gaze caught on a house or a horse or another car, and the detail sprang to life for her.

Just like her mind.

Ever since her session with Dr. Jim, a kaleidoscope of images and scenes had been shifting through her brain and occasionally, one would come into focus with sharp clarity. But her memories of Ryder remained cloudy.

"Doesn't look like Sheriff Ballard is here yet." Ryder pulled a U-turn at the end of the block and eased his truck in front of Julia's house.

Before getting out of the car, Julia pressed her nose against the cool glass of the window. Her heart skipped a beat. Someone had left her front gate ajar. She wiped her sticky palms on her jeans. Probably the mailman.

She shoved the car door open and tripped toward the swinging gate, with Ryder calling out behind her. If her secret admirer had left another bunch of scraggly flowers, she'd rip them to pieces.

Charging up the walkway, she frowned. Something on her porch. Her gait faltered and she swallowed. Not flowers. She stumbled on the first step. Something wet. Her breath hitched in her throat. Something red. She ground her fist against her mouth.

Blood.

Chapter Seven

The oozing, thick metallic smell gagged her, causing her knees to buckle. Strong arms caught her from behind.

"What the hell?" Ryder pulled her against his chest, and she sank against his tensed muscles.

His heart thundered against her shoulder blade, giving her strength, shoring her up. She straightened her spine and took a deep breath of cleansing mountain air.

Squeezing her shoulders, he nudged her off the step. "Wait here."

He crept up to the porch, avoiding drops of red liquid seeping into the wood. Hunching forward, he dabbed his finger at the streaks smeared across her front door and brought his finger to his nose.

"It's blood all right," he called over his left shoulder.

She figured that, but from what source? Her gaze darted around her small, fenced-in yard. Relief swept through her, knowing Shelby was safe with the McClintocks.

Ryder jogged down the steps, pulling a handkerchief from his jeans pocket. He wiped the blood from his fingers and grabbed Julia's arm with his other hand. "Let's wait outside the gate for Ballard."

"D-do you think there might be someone in my house?"

"I don't think so, but we don't want to touch anything else until the sheriff gets here."

He steered her onto the road in front of her house just as the sheriff wheeled up in his squad car.

"Are you waiting for me?" He waved a CD above his head. "I got it right here."

Julia's stomach clenched. She'd forgotten about that other nightmare looming in the shadows—her ex-husband's clandestine activities.

Ryder held out his hand. "Yeah, but we've got another problem. Looks like Julia's stalker paid another visit."

Sheriff Ballard shoved the CD into Ryder's hand as if anxious to get rid of it. "More flowers?"

"Worse."

"Not another break-in?" Ballard scowled. "We don't need an uptick in the crime statistics during the height of the summer season."

"Don't worry, Sheriff." Ryder waved his hand toward the blood-splattered porch. "This is a one-man crime wave."

"Hell and damnation." Ballard hitched up his pants and gingerly walked a semicircle in front of Julia's porch. "Looks like blood."

"It is blood." Ryder held up his right index finger. "I sampled a little from the lower-left corner of the door."

"Anything dead around here?" Ballard twisted his head over his shoulder to scan the front yard.

Julia cleared her throat. "Not that we noticed."

Ballard blew out a breath. "Too bad you don't have any neighbors, Julia. I suppose there aren't any witnesses. Are the Fourniers your closest neighbors?"

"Closer than Gracie and Charlie, but don't you think they

would've called you if they'd seen somebody on my porch spreading blood all over my front door?"

"You have a point, but I'll drive up the road to see if they noticed anything unusual. We'll dust for prints here and take a sample of that blood, and then you can clean up this mess."

"Seems I have a lot of messes to clean up lately." She shoved her hands in her pockets and kicked her toe at the ground. She wanted to catch this maniac red-handed, literally. Her memories and her old life hovered within her grasp and she wanted to take hold with both hands and banish the fear and uncertainty that had dogged her since the accident. She didn't need another complication.

Another patrol car pulled in front of Sheriff Ballard's, and Zack Ballard popped his head up over the open door. "Have you been looking for me…Sheriff?"

"Yeah, I wanted you to run something over here to Julia, but I couldn't bring you up on the radio."

Zack hunched over the car door, leaning on his folded arms. "I had it on. Just heard a little static earlier, but no call."

"Doesn't matter now. We have another problem. Julia's secret admirer left her another gift, a gory one."

"Stalker." Julia clenched her jaw.

"Excuse me, honey?"

Why did the men in this town always use sweet little endearments for her? Bet nobody ever called Julia Rousseau of Paris *honey*. "Secret admirers don't leave gifts of blood. This guy's a stalker, and I think he's dangerous."

"Blood?" And all of the same drained from Zack's face. "Someone left blood? From what?"

"I'm presuming an animal, but we haven't found anything yet." Ballard jerked his thumb over his shoulder. "We'll take a sample and prints, if we find any."

Ryder had been slowly moving toward Zack's squad car, and now he bent over, pointing at the front right bumper. "Is this blood?"

Zack's head jerked up. "On my bumper?"

"Take a look."

Julia followed Sheriff Ballard out to the road and leaned over Ryder's shoulder. A red smear with brown fur sticking to it clung to the chrome bumper.

"What is that, boy?" Sheriff Ballard straightened up and drilled Zack with a steely gaze.

"I must've hit that animal." Zack's eyes shifted between the three faces turned toward him. "I came down this way earlier on my way to Gracie Malone's B and B. Some small animal ran into the road in front of my car. I thought I missed him, but I guess not. Must've grazed him at least."

"Where was this?"

Ryder's lips formed a thin line, and Julia's heart skittered in her chest. He didn't really think Zack had a hand in this, did he?

"I don't know. Somewhere back toward Gracie's." Zack waved an ineffectual arm behind him.

"Will you show me?" Without waiting for an answer, Ryder climbed into Zack's squad car.

Zack and his father exchanged glances, and Sheriff Ballard nodded almost imperceptibly.

As the car crawled onto the road, Julia turned back to her violated house. "Are you going to get your evidence so I can clean up?"

"I'll get my kit out of the car." The sheriff grabbed his door handle and hesitated. "You don't think Zack had anything to do with this, do you, Julia?"

She shrugged. "You said you couldn't raise him on the radio before. Where was he?"

"I don't know." Sheriff Ballard clenched his jaw. "But don't worry. I'll find out."

Zack Ballard didn't seem like the stalking sort, but what did she know? She'd obviously married a man who turned traitor, a man who hit her, a man willing to threaten his so-called friend and colleague.

She opened her garage door and grabbed a bucket, a scrub brush, some detergent and a bottle of bleach. Once Ballard finished with her porch and door, she'd have to go inside, but the thought made her stomach twist in knots. Had the madman continued his sick pranks in her house?

When she rounded the corner, Ballard was standing back from the porch, clutching two evidence baggies and frowning.

"What is it?" She dropped her cleaning supplies on the ground.

"Someone left you a message in the blood."

"What's the message? Leave or die? That's what he left on Ryder's truck."

"No, I think he wrote that message for Ryder." Ballard scratched his jaw. "This message is for you—*You're mine.*"

A chill snaked up her spine, but she shook it off and tossed back her hair. "Yeah, right. That's the way to a woman's heart. Don't say it with diamonds, say it with blood."

Sheriff Ballard cocked his head. "Are you all right? I'm thinking the next step here is to install a camera outside your house. Next time this Romeo comes calling, we'll catch him in living color."

Julia opened her mouth to respond when Zack's squad car pulled up to the curb, and Ryder hopped out holding a soiled rag. Did he find that in Zack's car?

"We found the spot where Zack hit the animal on the road, but the animal is gone. I mopped up some of the blood with this cloth, so you can test it against the blood on Julia's porch."

Zack walked to the front of his car and leaned against the hood. "Looks like someone came along, scooped up the animal I hit and smeared its blood on Julia's door. Wouldn't you say, Ryder?"

Julia told Ryder about the message on the door and Sheriff Ballard's suggestion to install a camera.

Ryder's lips tightened and a dark flame flared in his eyes when she told him what the stalker had written.

"You are not going to stay here tonight."

"Nonsense." She scooped up the bucket and swung it from her hand. "I'm not allowing some nut who plays with roadkill to scare me out of my house."

"What about Shelby?"

Julia stopped and the bucket banged against her shin. "I don't want her here."

"Exactly. She can stay with my family. You can, too."

"I think if she's going to stay with anyone, it should be the Stokers. She knows them better than your parents, Ryder, and I can't quite imagine your dad being happy with a little girl in the house."

"Let's discuss this later." He tilted his chin toward the Ballards, taking pictures of the mess on the porch. Then he helped her measure detergent in the bucket and fill it with water.

"Okay, we have what we need." Sheriff Ballard patted the bag hanging over his shoulder. "There's not much evidence here, but once you get that camera up we'll nail him."

"Just look for someone toting a dead animal carcass around. Shouldn't be too hard to spot." Ryder pointed at Zack's bumper. "You might want to clean off your car, Ballard."

When the two squad cars drove out of sight, Julia turned to Ryder. "Do you think it's Zack?"

"I didn't see any blood in his car or on his uniform. If he hit the animal and then picked it up to use its blood to decorate your house, there should've been some sign of it."

"He went missing. Maybe he had time to go home and shower."

"If he took that much time, you'd think he would've wiped the blood off his bumper." Ryder grabbed the scrub brush from her hand and charged toward the porch.

She laughed. "This is Zack Ballard we're talking about."

"I'm glad you can laugh about it." He grinned at her. "How'd we miss that message on the door?"

"It's small." She pointed to the words smudged out in the blood, and felt a thrill of victory when her finger didn't tremble.

Ryder sloshed the soap in the bucket of water and doused the porch with it. He crouched forward and began scrubbing the stains from the wood.

"Did you ever go inside the house?"

"Not yet." She aimed the nozzle of the hose at the bottom of the step and shot a spray of water that carried the red-tinged soap in a tide down the walkway and into the grass.

"Don't you think you should take a look?" He dipped the brush in the bucket again and sat back on his heels. "I'm surprised Sheriff Ballard didn't have you check inside."

"I think Sheriff Ballard was a little worried that I might find more evidence linking his son to these…tricks."

"Maybe that's why he suggested the camera. He meant it as a warning to Zack. Let's finish up here, and I'll go inside with you."

Ryder scrubbed and she rinsed, and they vanquished most of the red streaks and drops. She stepped back, hands on her hips. "I'm going to have to paint that door. Maybe I'll paint it red this time to save myself the trouble next time."

Ryder dropped the brush and peeled off the rubber gloves. "There's not going to be a next time, even if I have to stake out your place myself."

She liked the sound of that, but her mouth quirked at the irony. Just when she found a man ready and willing to protect her, she'd rediscovered her backbone. Knowing more about her past and what she'd survived gave her courage. After escaping from her traitorous ex-husband and his killers, she didn't fear a garden-variety stalker. Did she?

"Are you ready?" Ryder gestured toward the newly scrubbed front door.

Julia tried the handle first and blew out a breath when she discovered the lock engaged. She inserted her key and pushed the door open, but Ryder stepped in front of her, shielding her with his solid form.

She trailed after him through the house as he checked every room and every closet. Looked like the new, heavy-duty locks kept the weirdo out this time.

"Now that we've resolved one issue, can I have a look at this on your computer?" Ryder waved the CD that he'd shoved in his jacket pocket at her.

Julia swallowed. Cleaning up the mess hardly resolved the problem of her stalker, and now they had to move onto the next issue. This one would be easier to handle. At least the disc never made it into the hands of the bad guys and now it looked like it never would.

She led Ryder to her computer where he sat down and inserted the CD. The computer allowed him to access the CD and even open the file, but that's where it stopped. Lines of symbols ran across the document, which was locked for editing.

Ryder peered at the screen and grunted. "That's ours. Jeremy must've stolen this CD from Black Cobra and hidden it in your apartment in Paris. When he was ready to sell it to our enemies, he called you to bring it to him in Arizona."

"He hid it under a loose floorboard." Wedging her hip

against the chair, Julia caught her lower lip between her teeth. The Paris apartment flooded her senses—the gleaming hardwood floors, the way the sun spilled across the dining room table, the scent of roses that filled vases scattered across a brightly furnished room, the sea-green comforter that almost floated above the antique bed.

The bed. Love and warmth emanated from that bed, so strong Julia longed to sink into it, wrap herself in its pleasure. She must have loved Jeremy at one point. They shared that bed together as husband and wife.

No, not Jeremy.

"Do you remember?" Ryder looked up from the computer, his gaze searching her face.

His warm, blue eyes deepened the languid pleasure, throbbing in her veins at the memory of the bed in her Paris apartment. A surge of desire claimed her body, weakening her knees. Gripping the back of the chair, she sank against its arm, the side of her hip brushing Ryder's shoulder.

Ryder curled his arm around her waist and pulled her into his lap. With her legs dangling over the arm of the chair, Ryder kissed her mouth. His lips sought hers in a sweet caress, tentative, almost gentle.

She didn't want gentle. She craved the scorching, searing passion imprinted on her soul by...Ryder? She couldn't remember. She couldn't remember Ryder in her bed. Couldn't remember Ryder making love to her. She only knew she could feel it now. But what if the memories of that passion came from her ex-husband and not Ryder?

An iron vice fell from his heart. Julia remembered. She remembered their love, remembered how he'd helped her pick up the pieces of her life when she discovered Jeremy's betrayal of their wedding vows. Now he knew she hadn't thought of him as her rebound man, her second choice, forever the middle brother. She'd risked her life to save his by delivering the CD to Jeremy in Arizona.

She must realize their love created Shelby and she wasn't afraid. She was going to trust him to be a father to their daughter.

He deepened his kiss, but Julia stiffened in his arms. Her body, soft and compliant only seconds earlier, shot up straight and tense. Her legs flailed in the air as she tried to gain a foothold on the floor.

Planting her hands on his thighs, she launched out of the chair and stumbled against the desk. Her eyes widened while a range of emotions played in their depths.

"I'm sorry. The events of the day are taking their toll."

What just happened? He cocked his head to the side. Her actions convinced him she remembered their relationship and the heady days they spent in Paris after her divorce and before his reassignment to Somalia. Was she pushing him away because she knew he was Shelby's father?

"You said you remembered."

"I remembered about the disc." She shoved her hands in her pockets and spun around to face the window.

He gripped the arms of the chair. She remembered finding the CD, not making love with him. How important could it have been to her? Her memories were flooding in from all directions now, but she still didn't remember him.

"So you recall the phone call from Jeremy leading up to finding the CD under the floorboards?" He closed the coded file and ejected the CD.

"Not exactly. The conversation itself is gone, but I recall the urgency of getting that disc and bringing it to Jeremy."

Did the urgency come from protecting him or from doing Jeremy's bidding? Maybe Jeremy's killer interrupted his reconciliation with Julia or maybe it was Julia's pregnancy. Discovering her pregnancy must've enraged Jeremy.

Ryder shook his head. Could he start over with Julia if he'd only imagined the love they shared?

JULIA GLIDED into the living room with her finger to her lips. "I finally got Shelby to sleep. She couldn't stop talking about Skipper and the riding lesson."

"Glad she liked it." Ryder dropped his father's tools in the metal chest and rubbed his hands on the seat of his jeans. "She's a natural on horseback."

"Is the camera installed?" Julia gestured toward the toolbox.

"Cameras. I installed one on the front porch, hidden in a hanging flower pot and one on the back porch in another flower pot. Just don't give those two plants much water."

Julia's shoulders slumped as she sat on the arm of an overstuffed chair. The situation upset her more than she let on, which typified the Julia he knew. She put on a brave front even as she crumbled inside. He wanted to let her know she could crumble right in front of him and he wouldn't turn away, wouldn't run, wouldn't demand that she hold herself together like her mother would have. Like Jeremy would have.

"Are you going to be okay here tonight? I could stay."

"No." She sat up straight and a pink tide crept over her cheeks. "I'll be fine, and Shelby's with the Stokers now. I don't want to impose on you anymore. You've been spending all your time with me and Shelby since you've been home. I'm sure your family wants to see you."

"I wouldn't bet on that. They have the heir apparent, Rod, and the other prodigal son, Rafe, is coming home in a few days to stay." He picked up his hat and twirled it on his hand. "I meant the couch."

"What?"

"If I stayed the night, I'd sleep on the couch."

"Ryder, I…"

"You don't need to explain." He held up his hands. "It's been a long, busy day. I'll pick you up in the morning for your appointment with Dr. Brody."

"I've been thinking about what you said. I'm not sure he's the best therapist for me."

"Maybe you should tell him that tomorrow. In the meantime, get some sleep." All of his nerve endings tingled in a desire to take her into his arms and make love to her until she remembered every inch of his body, every inch she'd explored with a feverish passion.

He swallowed the hard lump in his throat. "Good night, Julia."

He leaned his forehead against the doorjamb until he heard her turn the deadbolt into place with a click. Then he expelled a long breath and jogged down her newly scrubbed front porch.

He slid into his truck, punched on the radio, and maneuvered the seat into a reclining position. Adjusting his hat low over his face, he settled his shoulders into the seat and stretched his legs out as far as they would go against the floorboard.

Sipping the soda he had swiped from Julia's fridge, he watched her house. Even if she didn't want him inside on her couch…or in her bed…he had no intention of abandoning the two most important people in his life.

Chapter Eight

Julia twitched the curtain back into place and tousled her bed-head hair. Would Ryder go back to the ranch and shower and change before picking her up for Durango or did he plan to camp out in front of her house the rest of the morning?

The warmth that started in her belly when she realized Ryder had kept watch in his truck all night engulfed other areas of her anatomy as she felt the full weight of her feminine power settle around her shoulders like a fur stole. She liked the protection he offered, but she loved the other offer in his dark blue eyes as his hungry gaze devoured her before he left last night.

She'd been crazy to refuse that invitation. Of course they shared feelings in the past. They probably never acted on those feelings because of Jeremy and her pregnancy. Maybe that's why Ryder wouldn't give her the details of their relationship. She'd been in a bad marriage and in love with another man—Ryder.

He was just waiting for her to remember. She could understand that, but she couldn't understand why she didn't remember Ryder. She knew him on a visceral level, but couldn't quite grasp the specific memories of their relationship.

She wedged a shoulder on the window sash and grinned as Ryder's truck sputtered to life and pulled away from the curb.

Maybe she'd get a handle on those memories today in her last session with Dr. Brody.

As soon as Ryder's truck disappeared around the bend, Charlie Malone's jeep careened around the corner and stopped in front of her house. He came around to the passenger side and opened the door. A leggy brunette, tugging at a thigh-high denim skirt tripped out of the car.

Julia swung open her door and stepped onto the porch. "Hey, Charlie."

"Hi, Julia." He lifted his hand before stuffing it into his pocket. "My mom sent me over to see if you needed any help."

"Help?" Her gaze slid to the woman, combing fingers through her long, brown hair, tangled from the ride in the convertible jeep. If this woman had stepped forward after Julia's accident, claiming to be her sister, Julia would have believed her.

Charlie waved an arm toward her house. "My mom saw Ryder doing some work on your house yesterday. She told me to drop by to lend a hand."

Julia compressed her lips, trying to tame her smirk. Lend a hand and find out why Sheriff Ballard was here. "Thanks, but we got everything done. Who's your friend?"

Charlie had always been awkward around women, dating only those his mother presented to him. This woman, with her black eyeliner and short skirt, didn't look like the type Gracie usually foisted on Charlie.

Charlie's face sported two red spots as he stepped to the side. "This is Rosie Fletcher. Rosie, this is Julia Sto…"

His words hung in the air. He didn't know what to call her now.

"It's Rousseau. Julia Rousseau." She extended her arm to Rosie, and they shook hands.

"Rosie works at our B and B. On my way over here from town, I saw her walking back to the B and B."

"That's a long walk from town. Did you walk all the way in, too?" Julia looked down at Rosie's dirty feet shoved into flimsy sandals with small jeweled heels.

"No, I hitched a ride from a local and couldn't find a ride back. Good thing Charlie came along." Rosie batted her long, dark eyelashes and rubbed Charlie's shoulder.

Julia raised her eyebrows. Charlie didn't stand a chance against this one, and Mama Malone would definitely not approve.

Rosie tilted her head. "Hey, it's true."

Warmth edged into Julia's cheeks under Rosie's bright stare. What did Rosie hear about her? "What's true?"

"We look alike. A few people have told me that since I arrived in Silverhill."

Julia let out a breath and smiled. "Yeah, I noticed."

"And I noticed you've been monopolizing that tall, gorgeous cowboy, Ryder McClintock, since he's been back. Are you going to give the rest of us girls a crack at him?"

Julia's mouth gaped open.

Rosie laughed. "Just kidding. I'm waitin' on his brother, Rafe, anyway. I've heard a few stories about him and if he looks anything like Ryder…" She winked and tucked her hand into Charlie's pocket.

"I—I guess if you don't need any help, we'll be seeing you." Charlie turned around, but not before Julia caught a glimpse of the dark scowl rolling across his face.

Julia shook her head. That girl had too many fingers in too many pies. She'd just better keep those sticky fingers off Ryder.

"SHOULD WE PRESS the buzzer like last time?" Ryder jerked his thumb at Dr. Brody's door, firmly closed.

"No, he has an appointment before mine today. When he's finished, he'll open the door."

"When are you going to tell him?"

"I'll wait until after the session." She bit her lip. She agreed with Ryder that Jim should have been able to help her recover her memories before now. Her suspicions of him grew after Ryder found out about his censure. She needed to move on.

"Maybe you should tell him before. Don't you need the session to work out transference or countertransference or whatever?"

"I never experienced any transference with Dr. Brody." She crossed her arms and perched on the arm of the leather love seat.

"Speak for yourself. I think Dr. Brody has a thing for you."

"And you really think that thing involves leaving flowers and blood on my porch?"

"I don't know." He lifted a shoulder and winced. "Maybe the cameras will tell us that."

"Did you hurt your shoulder?"

"My neck's a little stiff."

"From sleeping in your truck last night?" She pushed up from the love seat and prowled to his chair. Placing a hand on the top of his shoulder, she wiggled her fingers beneath his shirt where they met his smooth, warm skin.

"You noticed that, did you?" He closed his eyes and his head fell back.

"Hard to miss a big, white truck sitting outside my house with a cowboy lounging in the front seat." She kneaded a tight muscle where his neck and shoulder met, and he groaned.

"Just didn't want to leave you alone in that house after what happened."

"I should've let you stay inside. I'm sorry." Her fingers slid down the front of his shirt, splaying across the hard muscles of his chest.

He opened his eyes and grabbed her other hand, planting a kiss on her palm. "Don't be sorry. You need time, time to remember…"

"Sorry I'm late."

Dr. Brody burst through his office door, and Julia jumped back from Ryder as if she was sixteen and Dad just discovered her on the couch with a boy. Maybe Ryder had the right idea about that transference stuff.

She glanced over Dr. Brody's shoulder into his empty office. "Don't you have another patient?"

"Cancelled. I was just transcribing a tape from an earlier session. Are you ready?"

Dr. Brody's wide smile didn't mesh with his narrowed eyes, and Julia felt more confident than ever in her decision to end treatment with him.

"Do you think Ryder needs to be present again?" She glanced over her shoulder at Ryder and rolled her eyes.

"Of course he needs to be present." Dr. Brody swept his arm into his office.

As Julia brushed past him, he stiffened. Then he followed her into the office ahead of Ryder.

"Let's get right down to business. Feeling susceptible today, Julia?"

Jerk. Brody had a crush on Julia, and he'd been holding her back from making progress all these years because he didn't want to lose her to her memories of another life...another man. He had half a mind to report him even though it would be hard to prove. Of course, if Brody turned out to be Julia's stalker, they'd nail him for more than improper conduct.

As Brody's smooth voice flowed through the room, Julia's eyelids drooped and the hands she'd been clasping in her lap fell to her sides.

At least the guy had his methods of hypnosis down.

Julia's memories came easily now. She recalled her childhood with her parents, the loneliness of being an only child and shuttling between two countries. Her trust and love for her father shined through, as did her rancorous relationship with her mother.

Even her first meeting with Jeremy and the reasons for her attraction to him tumbled from her lips. After their separation and subsequent divorce, Julia had explained it all to him. How lost she felt after her father's death and how Jeremy's overwhelming and extravagant attention filled that void, making her whole again.

"But then the relationship soured, didn't it, Julia?"

She nodded. "When I met Jeremy, I had blinders on. He swept me away when I needed sweeping away. I didn't notice his faults, didn't want to notice his faults."

"Did you know he was involved in sabotage when you left him?"

"No." She screwed up her eyes. "Not then, but I found out he was cheating on me, and he got violent when I confronted him about it."

"So you paid him back by taking a lover of your own, didn't you?"

Ryder's head snapped up as he glared at Brody. What the hell was the man doing?

Brody held his hand out to him. His soothing voice took on a hard edge. "You had an affair while you were married, didn't you, Julia?"

"I loved Ryder." Sinking back against the cushions, Julia smiled. "I still love Ryder."

The tight knot in Ryder's belly unraveled and his doubts dissipated. She loved him and it had nothing to do with being on the rebound from Jeremy. Maybe Brody knew what he was doing, but he had a misconception about when their affair started. Julia never cheated on Jeremy.

"And you made love to Ryder while you were still married to Jeremy. Maybe that's why you can't remember him. It's the guilt."

Ryder clenched his jaw. Was Brody trying to help her regain her memory or make her feel like crap?

"No." A furrow gathered between Julia's eyebrows as she tilted her head. "We fell in love while I was still married to Jeremy, but we didn't get together until after the separation."

"Then why are you suppressing memories of Ryder? Is there some secret about your relationship?"

Ryder shifted in his seat. What kind of game was Brody playing? He'd obviously figured out Ryder was Shelby's father. Why was he pressing Julia now? Ryder wanted Julia to remember the pregnancy on her own, not like this. Growling from the back of his throat, he stood up, looming over Brody.

"You can't disturb her now unless you want to cause some damage to her psyche." Brody turned his smug smile on Ryder.

Ryder clenched his fist, ready to smash that smile to smithereens, but he didn't know a thing about hypnosis and he wouldn't do a thing to jeopardize Julia's safety.

"How about it, Julia? Are you keeping a secret from Ryder?"

"My pregnancy." A single tear rolled down Julia's face. "I found out I was pregnant with Ryder's baby before he left for his next mission, but I didn't want to tell him. I didn't want to hold him or trick him. He'd already told me he didn't want children."

Had he really said something so stupid? After meeting Shelby, he couldn't remember a time when he didn't want to have children, a perfect little tomboy with gleaming curls.

"So you hid the truth from Ryder, and he's been hiding the truth from you."

Ryder uncurled his fists and flexed his fingers. He'd strangle him instead.

"When Ryder walked back into your life on Silverhill's

main street and saw Shelby, he must've known she was his daughter. And he kept the truth from you. Why do you think he did that?"

"Stop it, Brody," Ryder said through clenched teeth.

"I don't know." Julia pinned her hands between her knees and began rocking.

"Maybe he lied to you because you lied to him. Maybe he has plans to take Shelby away from you, an unfit mother who has panic attacks, a black hole for a memory, and a dangerous man stalking her."

Ryder crouched behind Brody's chair and hooked an arm around his neck. He hissed in his ear, "Bring her out of it now, you piece of garbage. And when this is over, you'll have another black spot on your record with that psychology board."

Brody choked and clawed at Ryder's forearm. "Okay, okay."

Rubbing his throat, Brody intoned the words to bring Julia out of her hypnotic state. As he encouraged her to remember everything from the session, he shot a vindictive glance at Ryder, hovering at Julia's side.

Julia's eyelids fluttered open and she crossed her arms over her chest, gripping her upper arms. Her gaze slid from Brody's triumphant face to Ryder's tight one.

She sat forward, her wide eyes brimming with distrust. Ryder ran his hand down her back, but she bristled at his touch.

"I'd say that was a very successful session because you finally discovered the identity of Shelby's father." Brody snapped his notebook shut and stood up.

Ryder lunged for Brody and grabbed his shirt collar.

Julia yelled, "Stop. He's not worth it."

Ryder shoved him back and wiped his hands on the thighs of his jeans. "I'm filing a complaint against you."

Smiling, Brody straightened his shirt. "Go ahead. I didn't

record this session. It's one disgruntled…patient's word against mine. She was in a hypnotic state."

"I'm not coming back, Jim. It's over. I don't think you ever had my well-being as your top priority." Julia rose from the sofa and rubbed her pale, tear-smudged face.

"I protected you, Julia. People don't get amnesia just because of a bump on the head. You wanted to forget. I knew that. I spared you memories of a cheating spouse and a man who didn't want you or your child, and he proved that when he came waltzing back into your life. Why didn't he admit to being Shelby's father? Either he doesn't want her or he wants her all to himself. Think about it. Ryder McClintock showed up in town only a few weeks after the stalking incidents began. Maybe he's trying to drive you crazy so he can snatch Shelby away from you."

"That's enough." Ryder thrust his arm out as if to deflect Brody's words.

"You see, Julia. He's a violent man, just like your ex-husband. They're spies for goodness sakes. They live in a violent, turbulent world. You don't need that. Shelby doesn't need that."

Ryder pushed past him and threw open his office door, startling a man reading a magazine. How did Brody know Julia planned to call it quits with him before the session started? He had an agenda from the minute they walked into his office.

Ryder's trained eye scanned the room. He stood on a table and felt behind the speaker in the corner while Brody's next patient stared at him with an open mouth.

"What are you doing?" Julia hung back by Brody's office door while the doctor hovered over her shoulder, his brow wrinkled.

Ryder's fingers trailed along the top of a picture frame until they stumbled on a device tucked into the corner. He yanked out the mini camera and microphone and held it up.

"Spying on your patients before they even come into your office, Brody? I think that board of yours is going to be very interested in this." He dangled the camera from his fingertips, swinging it in front of the waiting patient. "Don't you think?"

The man tossed his magazine on the table and grabbed the doorknob. "What kind of office is this?"

"See ya, doc." Ryder pocketed the electronic device and followed the man out into the hallway.

Julia clicked the door behind her and leaned against it, closing her eyes.

"Julia, I wanted to tell you, but I wanted you to remember first. Of course I knew Shelby belonged to me the minute I saw her. You and Jeremy didn't even sleep together at the end of your marriage, and I knew damn well you wouldn't have gone back to him after I left."

"Shelby doesn't belong to you. She's mine." Julia shoved off the doorjamb and marched toward the elevator.

Ryder stared at her stiff back. Great. She misinterpreted his patience as deception. By giving her time to remember their love, he'd driven a huge wedge between them.

"I WANT another riding lesson with Ryder." Shelby planted her pink sneakers in the carpet and folded her arms.

"Not today, Shelby." Julia tossed a couple of water bottles in the backpack, followed by two granola bars, a light blanket and her cell phone.

"You promised. Ryder promised." Shelby thrust out her lower lip and bunched up her arms tighter.

"Promises get broken. People lie." Julia swung the backpack over her shoulder and stalked to the front door. A small sniffle stopped her dead in her tracks.

She ventured a look over her shoulder just in time to see

a big, fat tear wobble on the end of Shelby's lashes and her lip tremble.

Julia spun around and dropped to her knees in front of Shelby's shuddering frame. Folding her arms around her, she said, "I'm sorry, honey bun. Ryder's busy with his brother today. You'll have another riding lesson later this week. Ryder doesn't break his promises and he doesn't lie."

He just withholds information.

Julia wiped the tear from Shelby's face and took her hand. "Let's take our hike to The Twirling Ballerinas. When you have your sleepover at Clem and Millie's tonight, you can pick out one of the kittens."

Shelby's face brightened as she rubbed the back of her hand across her nose. "I want the black and white one."

"Okay. Clem will let us know when the kitty is ready to leave its mama."

Julia's grip tightened on Shelby's hand when they left the house and made their way toward the start of the trail.

"Too tight." Shelby shook her hand free of Julia's and skipped ahead.

Julia had to shed the fear that Ryder intended to steal Shelby from her. She knew her overprotection of Shelby bordered on smothering and she didn't want to be that kind of mother.

She'd grown accustomed to having Shelby all to herself. Her daughter represented her lifeline as she groped in the darkness of her past. She didn't want to share Shelby and only felt relief when she found out her ex-husband was dead and wouldn't be calling on her for visitation rights and joint custody.

But Ryder wasn't Jeremy. Again, once the hypnosis peeled back a corner on her memories, they poured forth in sweet, agonizing detail. She recalled her first meeting with Ryder when Jeremy brought him to their Paris apartment. The problems with Jeremy had already begun, and Julia and Ryder had shared many laughs that weekend that excluded a morose Jeremy. Electricity sizzled between them, the same connection she felt the first time she saw him on Silverhill's main street.

When she and Jeremy separated, Ryder had kept his distance, but the pull between them was too strong. Her skin tingled even now as she recalled making love with Ryder.

She remembered discovering her pregnancy as if it happened yesterday. She also remembered the uncertainty that plagued her. Wary of large families with pressing expectations, Ryder had told her many times he didn't want children.

So why did the knowledge of his paternity frighten her now? If he didn't want kids, why did she fear he'd snatch Shelby away from her?

Maybe her real fear was that he wouldn't. That he'd have no interest in his daughter at all.

Shaking her head, she hitched the backpack up on her shoulders. She didn't know what she wanted or what she feared.

"Slow down, Shelby."

Except Jim Brody. She feared him. After that disastrous session yesterday, Jim had left several messages on her answering machine. She and Ryder had barely spoken on the drive home, and he dropped her off with a world of questions unanswered between them. So when the phone rang after dinner, she left it for the machine to pick up. But instead of Ryder's voice, Jim's voice, slurred and alternately pathetic and demanding, spewed out of the answering machine. The background noise indicated he'd placed those calls from a bar. Jim, the former alcoholic, had fallen off the wagon.

The booze had loosened his tongue and his inhibitions. He rambled on about how he loved her and wanted to protect her from her dangerous past and the dangerous men in it. With each message he left, Julia became more and more convinced that he had left the flowers, slashed the tires and bloodied her porch. And the fire at the hotel? He was probably responsible for that, too.

She shivered to think of the number of times she'd been holed up in that office with him alone.

"Wait for me, Shelby." Shelby had the sure-footedness of a mountain goat, but Julia always liked to keep her in sight on the trail especially on this narrow pathway.

Shelby plopped down on a rock to wait for her before negotiating the only tricky part of the trail. Julia took Shelby's arm, pulling her up and in front of her while she gripped her waist. Single file they picked their way along the path that led to a sheer drop to their left for several feet.

A shadow fell across the trail and Julia peered up. A large boulder tumbled from the hillside to their right. She screamed and shoved Shelby forward where the path widened.

The boulder crashed into Julia's legs, knocking her off her feet. She teetered on the soft shoulder of the path until the gravel gave way beneath her sneakers and she slid off the side of the mountain.

Chapter Nine

"Mama!" Shelby screamed above her and then her small face floated at the edge of the crumbled precipice.

"Stay back, Shelby." Julia grasped the dry, scrubby bush growing out of the side of the rock and extended her toes to feel for a ledge. Emptiness gaped below her. "Get back on the trail."

Shelby sobbed, but her head disappeared from the side of the ledge. Julia swung her body forward and cycled her legs to find a foothold on the face of the rock. The soles of her sneakers slid against the rough slab, dislodging small plants and pebbles.

Her body swayed, and the bush she clung to dipped lower as a root pulled free from the crack. She held her breath, afraid to make a move. She hoped Shelby would just wait on the trail for someone to come. Would someone come in time to help her?

She'd tossed her cell phone in the backpack, but it might as well be on the moon. She couldn't risk reaching back with one hand to retrieve it.

Her shoulders ached and her hands stung from the prickly bush she clung to with all her strength. Another ledge extended about ten feet below her. If she let go and dropped onto this outcropping she might break her leg, but if she fell she could very well roll off and plunge another fifty feet to her death.

She inched her toe up the side of the rock and felt another scrubby plant to her right. She tested the plant with her foot, and it stayed in place. Gripping her lifeline, she hoisted up her body with her foot balanced on the plant. As she inched higher, she released one hand from the bush to reach for another one above it.

The plant below her right foot gave way, and her knee slammed against the rock as she grabbed for her secure handhold. A sob ripped through her throat.

Don't panic. Don't lose control.

She searched the rock with her left toe, finding an indentation. If she could use this hole to push up again, she could grab that higher, sturdier plant and get closer to the edge. She took a deep breath and tensed her muscles.

"Julia?"

"Ryder! Ryder, I'm down here. Where's Shelby?"

"Shelby's safe." Ryder's head appeared over the edge of the rock. "Oh my God. Julia, don't move."

"Don't worry. I don't plan on going anywhere." Her shoulders burned now and her bloody hands throbbed with pain, but she felt an insane joy at seeing Ryder's face hovering above her.

"Hang on for one more minute." His face disappeared and despair descended again like a heavy cloud of dust.

"Ryder, don't leave me!"

"I'm right here." His head popped back into sight. "I have a rope with me. I'm tying it into a lasso."

Julia closed her eyes and concentrated on the light breeze caressing her face. She didn't know how or why, but Ryder arrived just in time. He'd save her.

"Ready?"

Peering up at him, she called out, "Yes."

A circle of rope twirled down to her right. "Did that make it over you?"

"No, but I think I can reach it with my right hand."

"Don't. I'll try again."

The rope slithered up the wall of rock and then whistled as it flew toward her again. This time the rope landed around her shoulders.

"It worked."

"Okay, take one hand at a time and slip it through the rope. The object is to get the rope under your arms and hold on to it. I'll yank the lasso tight and then pull you up. Can you do that?"

"Yes." She uncurled her hand from the scrubby plant, slid it through the circle of rope and then grasped the line leading straight to Ryder. "Okay, that's one."

Holding on to the rope was more secure than the bush, so she had an easier time with the second hand. With the rope encircling her body underneath her arms and both hands holding on to it, she called up, "I'm ready."

The lasso tightened around her. Even if Ryder had disappointed his parents with his ranching skills, he had a handle on this cowboy stuff.

"I'm going to start hauling you up now. Scream and yell if there's a problem and hold on to the rope."

Julia braced her feet against the rock and as Ryder pulled up the rope, she walked up the side of the cliff. She arrived at the top and Ryder scooped his arms beneath hers and yanked her over to solid ground.

She collapsed on top of him and they lay together, their breath escaping in short spurts. Ryder tightened his arms around her and she rested her cheek against his chest, listening to the echo of his thundering heart.

When her lungs stopped hurting, she raised her head. "We have to get off of this trail. Where's Shelby?"

He rolled to his side and pointed to where the trail widened. Shelby sat on a log and waved.

Julia lurched to her knees, the tears flowing down her face. Ryder helped her up and she rushed to Shelby's side and gathered her in her arms.

Ryder followed and crouched beside the log. "Shelby found me up the trail and brought me back here. She's amazing."

"I told you to wait, Shelby." Julia buried her head on Shelby's back. She didn't want her daughter to see her crying. Shelby had already witnessed too many of her mother's breakdowns.

"I waited, but I heard whistling. I knew it was Ryder. I knew Ryder would help you, Mama."

"And he did." She wiped her hands across her cheeks and turned to face Ryder. "He saved me. What were you doing up here?"

"I knew you took this hike almost every morning, so I waited for you at The Twirling Ballerinas. I wanted to talk." He took her hands and turned them over. He ran a light fingertip over her scratched and bleeding palms. "And it's a damn good thing I did. Let's walk back and treat your cuts. Are you hurt anywhere else?"

"Just a few bruises."

Ryder hoisted Shelby on his shoulders and rested his hand on Julia's hip as they picked their way back over the trail where the boulder fell. Julia glanced up at the rocks. The sun had crept up higher in the sky since the rock had knocked her over the cliff, but right before she heard it rumble, a shadow passed over the sun. The rock was falling downward. It couldn't have blocked out the sun on its descent.

Julia stumbled and Ryder grabbed her waist. "Steady, just a few more steps."

When the trail widened, Julia spun around and lifted Shelby from Ryder's shoulders. "Go pick some flowers and we'll put them in a vase when we get home."

Shelby scampered ahead and dived head first into the field of summer blooms.

"I'm glad to see the incident didn't scare her." Ryder tilted his chin toward Shelby rolling in a mass of petals.

"Didn't scare her, but I'm even more frightened now than when I was dangling in space. Ryder, someone pushed that boulder off the cliff, someone waiting for us."

Ryder's eyebrows shot up. "How do you know? Did you see someone?"

"I saw a shadow before the rock fell. Someone was up there and he wanted to kill me…us." Her knees started to tremble and she sank onto a boulder, similar in size and shape to the one some monster pushed toward her and Shelby.

Kneeling next to her, Ryder clasped her hand in his. The warmth and steadiness of his grip calmed her nerves.

Why did she push him away yesterday? He had his reasons for keeping quiet about their relationship. She should have given him an opportunity to explain.

When she first saw him on Main Street, a tiny hope flared that she'd found her long-lost husband and Shelby's father. One of those scenarios had come true. She should be thrilled Ryder turned out to be Shelby's father and not Jeremy. Shelby had a father to fill her with pride.

"When I get you two home, I'm coming back up here to have a look." Ryder waved his hand toward the jagged rocks above the trail.

"I guess my secret admirer doesn't admire me anymore." She rubbed her arms to quell the shiver stealing across body.

Ryder squinted into the sun. "If he can't have you, he wants to make sure nobody else does."

RYDER SETTLED Julia and Shelby at the house. Now that Julia's stalker had taken his show on the road, he could avoid the cameras. Who knew about the cameras besides Zack Ballard and Dr. Jim Brody? Hell, anyone hiding out with a pair of binoculars could've watched him install the cameras.

He tramped back up the trail, a slow blaze kindling in his gut. Julia had pissed off this maniac by not cherishing his pathetic gifts and then made things worse by keeping company with him.

Not that it mattered. The man stalking Julia had a tenuous hold on reality. There wasn't much she could've done to appease him. Any action on her part would have resulted in the same outcome. The man wanted her or he wanted her dead.

Before the main trail narrowed, a smaller trail forked to the right, leading up to the craggy rocks and crevices that overlooked Silverhill. Ryder scrambled over the first rock to take this alternate route.

He crept along the trail, hunched over, peering at the foliage along the sides. Judging by the snapped twigs and crushed leaves, someone had recently climbed this trail, but imprints of hiking boots and running shoes criss-crossed each other, obscuring any clear set of footprints.

He reached the outcropping of rocks that rose above the narrow path of the trail below. Moist earth and moss marked the spot where the boulder had come loose. He examined the area and found a broken board. Had Julia's attacker used that as leverage to dislodge the boulder?

Peering over the edge, Ryder had a clear view of the trail. The man loosened the boulder and then waited for Julia and Shelby. Ryder's jaw tightened along with his fists. He had to protect Julia and their daughter from this madman. He had to take him out before he did any more damage.

He stirred the dried leaves on the ground with his foot. The corner of a shiny object appeared in the dirt. Ryder pounced on it, feeling like those old prospectors must've felt almost a hundred and fifty years ago when they struck a vein of silver ore in these hills.

Pinching his find between two fingers, Ryder shook the dirt from it. He cradled the rectangular silver case in his palm and then pressed a small release lever. The lid to the case popped open, revealing a stack of thick cards embossed with gold letters: *Dr. James Brody, Licensed Clinical Psychologist.*

Ryder clutched the incriminating case in his hand so tightly, it bit into his flesh. He had all the proof he needed to get Brody out of Julia's life for good. And if he couldn't count on law enforcement to lock him up, well, he had his own methods.

Shoving the card case in his back pocket, he clambered over the rocks and dropped back onto the trail. Once they dealt with this freak, he and Julia could discuss their daughter and their future…together.

BY THE TIME Julia placed the last bunch of wildflowers in a vase, Shelby had crashed on the sofa. She slipped off Shelby's shoes and carried her to the pink princess bed. Positioning a pillow beneath Shelby's head, Julia studied her daughter's face.

She thought she'd memorized every detail, but now she noticed long lashes tipped with gold, like Ryder's. How had she missed the resemblance between her daughter and the man who came to Silverhill to save her? Had she really missed it or had she stuffed the creeping realization that Shelby was McClintock through and through deep into the shadows of her mind?

Now the truth screamed at her from all sides. The electricity between her and Ryder from the first moment he touched her. Ryder's interest and obvious pleasure in Shelby's company. Shelby's own comfort in Ryder's presence.

She'd been a fool.

Even Dr. Brody figured out the connection between Ryder and Shelby or maybe he just imagined it in his paranoid state. How many other people in Silverhill realized the truth about Shelby's paternity? She knew it wouldn't take long for word to spread.

The latch on her front gate squeaked and Julia peeked through a gap in the curtains. Ryder strode up her walkway, a frown marring his handsome features. Guess he didn't find anything. Sheriff Ballard wouldn't be sending any search parties out for a phantom.

She opened the door before he had a chance to knock. "You didn't find anything."

"Wrong." He slid his fingers into the back pocket of his jeans and pulled out a small, silver rectangle.

"What is it?" Her pulse ticked up a few notches. She hadn't imagined that shadow over the sun.

Ryder flicked the case open and held it out.

A dull pain throbbed behind her eyes. Despite his unethical behavior and frantic phone calls last night, Julia had a hard time believing Jim had been stalking her. Now the proof swam before her eyes in black and white, or rather, gold and white.

"He must be out of his mind. Why would he risk everything, his career, his reputation?"

"You said it. Out of his mind. I'm calling Ballard right now, and he'll contact the Durango Sheriff's Department. I don't know if this will be enough proof to arrest him, but it's going to put a serious crimp in his skulking."

"The phone calls." Julia pointed to her answering machine. "Jim left several messages last night, desperate, drunken, rambling messages."

"Why didn't you call me?"

"I—I didn't want to talk to you last night." A dark cloud passed over Ryder's face and his pain sliced her heart. "I wasn't ready…last night."

Almost two hours later, after Sheriff Ballard came over and collected the card case and the tape from the answering machine and took Julia's statement, she collapsed on the sofa. "It's over. Dr. Brody won't be able to hide from the Durango Sheriff's Department."

"Are you ready to talk now?" Ryder propped his shoulders against the doorjamb and folded his arms. "We have a lot to clear up, a lot to remember."

"I have a better idea." Julia curled her legs beneath her. "Shelby's going to a sleepover tonight at the Stokers' with their granddaughter. I'll cook dinner for you, and we can figure all this out."

"You cook?"

"I know I never cooked before, but I learned a few tricks since coming to Silverhill."

"You remember?"

"Yeah, I do."

From the wicked smile breaking across Ryder's face, he was recalling a lot more than her inability to cook. She didn't have to tell him she remembered their torrid affair. She planned to show him.

And that's exactly what the old Julia would do.

RYDER SHOWED UP for dinner, clutching a bottle of French wine in one hand and a six-pack of beer in the other. Good thing Rod installed a wine cellar at the house and stocked it with pretentious labels. Julia always loved a good bottle of Bordeaux.

She opened the door a crack before swinging it wide, and he almost dropped the bottle of wine on the ground. A slip of a summer dress skimmed Julia's curves and her dark hair danced along her shoulders, free of its customary ponytail.

"I come bearing gifts." He thrust the bottle in front of him.

She snatched the wine from his hand and peered at the label. "Impressive, but the old Julia is not quite up to full speed. I don't drink much anymore, not enough to do justice to this bottle. I didn't need alcohol fuzzing up my already fuzzy brain."

"Keep it for when Julia number one makes her triumphant return. Rod won't miss the bottle. I take that back. He probably keeps an inventory of the wine cellar, but that's tough luck for him."

"Ryder, what if Julia number one never completely returns? I'm not the stylish, madcap, rich girl living among sophisticates in Paris anymore."

"I know." He clunked the six-pack on her kitchen counter, and placed his hands on her shoulders. "You're the mother of my child."

"About that."

He ran a thumb along her jaw line. "We have time to work it out. If you haven't noticed I'm crazy about Shelby, but you're her mother and you know what's best for her. I'll follow your lead."

His confidence in his ability to win Julia back and gain the love and trust of his daughter gave him the luxury of making that concession. Julia would never shut him out of Shelby's life, and he had to make sure she'd never shut him out of her life, either.

Julia's face brightened. "Well, then, follow my lead to the kitchen. You can toss the salad while I put the finishing touches on my teriyaki chicken. It's better when I grill it outside, but…"

Her eyes shifted to the back door that led to a wooden deck and she shrugged. "No word yet?"

"The Sheriff's Department will find Brody, if they haven't already. He must know they're looking for him. He's not going to show his face around here again, especially with the cameras watching."

"You're right." She shook her head and her silky hair caught the recessed lights over the counter.

He wanted to run his fingers through her shimmering tresses, but she had to make the first move. He dumped the chopped vegetables into a big bowl of lettuce and inexpertly wielded a long wooden fork and spoon to toss the contents.

Julia snorted. "We went out to eat a lot, didn't we?"

"No, actually, I was an expert chef in Paris, studied at Le Cordon Bleu and whipped up fancy cuisine for you all the time."

"Yeah, right. Once all my memories start rolling in, you're going to have some explaining to do." She shoveled some rice from a rice cooker into a bowl and then spun around. "What happened to the CD? In all the…er…excitement, I forgot to ask you."

"I sent it to the Black Cobra offices in Washington."

"Black Cobra has offices in Washington? I thought it was a top secret agency."

"It is. The offices are as bland as any other government agency office."

"Have they gotten back to you yet?"

"I doubt Black Cobra is going to tell me the contents of the CD, but they did verify it's one of theirs. Jeremy breached security and stole it."

"Stand-up guy, my ex-husband."

"Don't start beating yourself over the head again because you married Jeremy. You already did that. The guy could charm a snake out of a basket, and you were vulnerable. He fooled everyone, not just you, and you're not even a top secret agency like Black Cobra. Imagine how Jeremy's employer felt when he turned."

"As foolish as I do."

He chucked her under the chin. "More. After all, you had Jeremy's number before Black Cobra did."

"I fell for Dr. Brody's act, too." She bit her nail and wrinkled her nose. "Seems I don't have very good judgment when it comes to men."

He didn't plan on touching that one even with the long fork he still clutched in his hand. Lifting his shoulders, he continued tossing.

Julia set the table and placed a small vase in the middle containing the wildflowers Shelby picked earlier. Ryder took his place across from her and expelled a long breath. Ever since he walked back into Julia's life, they'd been on a carousel of emotions thanks to Brody. With the danger behind her, Julia could come to terms with Shelby having a father in the picture.

"Do you want one of those beers you brought? Or the wine?" She half rose from her chair.

"I don't like to drink alone. Put the beers in the fridge for another time, and we'll save the wine for when we have something to celebrate—maybe your lack of fuzziness."

"I'm ready to banish the fuzziness right now." She took a gulp of water. "I planned to tell you about the pregnancy, Ryder. I was waiting for the right moment. You warned me you didn't want a family, and I didn't know how to break it to you."

"I was an ass. My views on family life made it hard for you to tell me. I get that."

"Then I got that call from Jeremy."

"You should've told me about that call."

"You'd just left for your next assignment. I knew any correspondence I sent wouldn't reach you for a few months and it would be heavily censored when it did."

He stabbed a piece of chicken with his fork. That's what he liked about his job. It could take months before he got any news from his family. Knowing this, they rarely contacted him about so-called family emergencies. He could remain blissfully out of the loop, but he didn't want to be out of Julia's loop.

He volunteered for another two years in the field when his attempts to reach Julia failed. He should've tried harder to find her. His compulsion to step back from entanglements had cost him big time. Had almost cost him his daughter.

"So you set off for Arizona by yourself to deliver the CD to Jeremy."

"I did it to…" A pink tide ebbed across her cheeks. "I did it to protect you."

"Black Cobra would've handled any fallout from that CD. Didn't you realize Jeremy would go crazy when he saw you pregnant?"

Julia pushed a few grains of rice around her plate. "I didn't think he'd care."

"You really didn't know Jeremy well, did you?"

"No. After the whirlwind courtship, I discovered I'd married a stranger. And he's still a stranger. I can't quite recall the night of the explosion." She picked up his empty plate. "Would you like more chicken?"

"Yeah. That was great." He noticed the crease between her brows. The events of the past few weeks had put her nerves to the test and she needed a break. And so did he. "Could you please bring me one of those beers and then tell me about Shelby? Show me her baby pictures. Tell me about her birth. Her first smile. Her first tooth. Her first word. Everything."

She set his plate and a bottle of beer in front of him. "You really want to know?"

"Everything."

He twisted off the cap on his beer and then sawed into his third piece of chicken, never imagining he'd ever eat anything Julia Rousseau cooked.

For the next hour and a half Julia filled him in on the details of Shelby's life. They'd moved from the table to the sofa where she pulled out photo albums and her laptop to show him hundreds of pictures of Shelby.

He studied each picture as if committing it to memory. He laughed, asked questions and marveled at Shelby's brilliance. In short, he acted like a proud papa.

Excitement fizzed along Julia's veins like a fine sparkling wine from Rod's cellar. Ryder wanted to be Shelby's father. Did he want more?

Only one way to find out.

Julia stood up and stretched, tousling her hair and raising her arms above her head. The light material of her sundress whispered around her thighs and pulled tightly across her breasts.

Ryder's gaze, glued to the laptop screen for the past fifteen minutes, shifted to Julia, dipped to her legs and then skimmed up her body, catching on her breasts.

His Adam's apple bobbed and his eyes widened.

A smile tugged at the corner of Julia's mouth. She hadn't lost her touch.

"Another beer?" She bent over at the waist, giving him an eyeful of her cleavage, and swept up his empty bottle from the coffee table.

"No, thanks."

"That's good." She twirled around and headed for the kitchen, swaying her hips, feeling Ryder's gaze hitched to every swing.

"Good? Why is that good?"

She plunked the bottle down on her kitchen counter and then sashayed her way back to the living room. "I don't want you to be impaired while you…" Ryder's eyebrows disappeared under a shock of sun-streaked brown hair "…drive home."

Licking his lips, he dug his elbows into his thighs and hunched over the laptop again.

Julia dropped onto the sofa next to him, wiggling her hips to scoot in closer. Her fingers played across the broad slabs of muscle on his back outlined by his T-shirt. Then she flicked them through the curls at the nape of his neck. "It's been a long time."

He snapped the laptop shut on Shelby's dimpled smile. "You're playing with fire, Julia."

"Maybe I want to get burned."

He twisted toward her, capturing both of her wrists in one large hand. "Prepare to get scorched."

Leaning forward, he took possession of her lips in a kiss so hot that she could've sworn the coral nail polish on her toes melted. Did she really think she could call the shots and control the tempo with Ryder McClintock? The man always knew what he wanted…and took it.

Better yet, he knew what she wanted.

And right now, his warm hand with its rough finger pads moving up her thigh hit the spot precisely. He pulled her into his lap and angled his mouth over hers, deepening the kiss. Reaching beneath his shirt, she trailed her fingernails along his sides and splayed her hand across his flat, hard belly.

A breath hitched in his throat and he pulled her lower lip between his teeth. When Ryder kissed her, really kissed her, the sensation lasted for days. That, she remembered.

She slipped two fingertips just inside the waistband of his

jeans. In response, he slid his hand into her panties, cupping her bottom. Always had to do her one better.

His mouth lingered on hers for a moment longer before his tongue teased her earlobe. Arching her back, she brushed her breasts against his solid chest. Ryder hooked a finger around the strap of her sundress and dropped it off her shoulder. He planted a path of kisses down her neck, sending a shaft of pleasure to her toes. She shuddered, a moan escaping from her lips.

"Do you remember everything now?" He caressed her cheek, his blue eyes darkening with passion.

"Everything about you," she breathed out, curling her arms around his neck.

Apparently she had the right answer. Ryder pushed up from the sofa, lifting her in his arms as if she weighed as little as one of those kittens Shelby wanted.

She wrapped her legs around his waist as he carried her into the bedroom and tossed her on top of the new bedspread.

She snorted. "Are you in a hurry or something?"

"You had the luxury of not remembering what you were missing all these years." He yanked his T-shirt over his head and dropped it on the floor. "While I dreamed about you every night."

She drank in his bare chest, all hard angles and flat planes. His biceps bunched in knots as he reached forward and unbuckled his belt. It gaped open and Julia's gaze snagged on the bulge in his jeans. Those must've been some dreams he had.

He sat on the edge of the bed and pulled off one boot. As he struggled with the second, she heaved an impatient sigh and scrambled off the bed. She landed in front of him and tugged at the stubborn boot. With a final pull she tumbled backward, landing on her bottom, Ryder's boot in her lap.

Laughing, Ryder pulled off his socks and tossed them over his shoulder. "Never helped a man with his boots before?"

"You never wore cowboy boots in Paris." She tossed the boot over her shoulder and prowled toward Ryder on her hands and knees.

His lids dropped half-mast over his eyes, as he leaned back on the bed on his elbows. Julia crawled forward and settled between his legs. She unfastened his jeans now tight over his crotch, and his erection tented his plaid boxers.

She ran her hand over his hard desire and swallowed. How could she have ever forgotten? He stood up, and she pulled down his jeans and underwear over his muscled thighs.

"Come on up here." His husky voice sent a ripple of longing down her back.

He encircled her waist with his hands, and she stood on her tiptoes to press the length of her body along his. The warmth of his bare skin seeped through the thin material of her sundress.

"Did you learn modesty somewhere along the line?"

She shook her head, and Ryder reached around and tugged down her zipper. The dress fell from her body with a whisper, and Ryder pulled her back into his arms as if he couldn't bear to have any space between them.

Then he fell backward on the bed, bringing her along. She shimmied out of her panties and straddled his hips. She leaned forward, her body hovering above his, and whispered, "I'm ready for my riding lesson now."

"You don't need lessons, babe, just a refresher course." A big grin split his face. "But before you take me for a ride, I'm going to take you for a ride."

Gripping her waist, he flipped her onto her back and skimmed his erection between her breasts and along her belly. His lips followed the same path, and Julia lifted her hips in anticipation of his sweet caress.

As his mouth met her heated flesh, she dug her heels into

his buttocks. The memories flooded her mind as the sensations flooded her body. Ryder had put her first. He always had.

Her fingers clawed through his hair as he took her to a precipice as high as the Colorado Rockies that loomed majestically outside her window. Her climax ripped through her, and while her muscles still clenched in wave after wave of pleasure, Ryder entered her. Julia squeezed her eyes shut in an attempt to wring every ounce of joy from the feeling of completeness Ryder gave her.

"Open your eyes," Ryder commanded in a guttural voice.

Her lids flew open and her eyes met Ryder's fierce gaze. His breath hissed between his teeth as he drove into her. He growled his release and she folded around him, never wanting to let go.

Later, Julia curled up against his side, her fingers playing across his collarbone. She landed a kiss on his shoulder. "How could I have ever forgotten that? Forgotten you?"

"Brody was wrong about a lot of things, but I think he hit the nail on the head with this one. I had already come back into your life. You felt less urgency to remember me."

"Maybe. Now our time together is all I can think about. All I want to think about."

"My thoughts are running in one single direction right now. Ready for the refresher course?"

"Mmm." She trailed her tongue along his throat, savoring his salty, masculine taste.

The phone on the nightstand interrupted her single-minded course and she pulled away from the feast in front of her. "I have to get this in case it's the Stokers. Shelby gets homesick sometimes."

She fumbled for the phone across Ryder's chest. "Hello?"

"Julia, this is Sheriff Ballard. I have some interesting news for you about Dr. Brody."

"You found him?" She bolted upright.

"Yeah, we found him all right. At the bottom of the gorge off Highway 160."

Chapter Ten

The rosy flush on Julia's face faded to white. Ryder smoothed her hair back from her cheek and mouthed the words, "What's wrong?"

She held up her hand to him. "I—is he dead?"

Brody was dead? Relief surged through his body. He couldn't help it. The proof they had against Brody didn't amount to much, and Ryder didn't want the doctor out on the streets.

"Uh-huh, I see." She clutched the phone in her hands, her knuckles as white as her face.

Ryder couldn't take the suspense anymore. He snatched the phone from Julia's stiff fingers. "Ballard, this is Ryder. What's going on?"

"Dr. Brody's car went off the road on Highway 160 and plunged into the gorge. He's dead."

"Do you think he did it on purpose?"

"I don't know. The Colorado State Patrol just recovered the car and his body. No autopsy or accident report yet. I'll keep you posted. By the way, you know your brother graduated from the police academy today and is coming home day after tomorrow, don't you?"

"Yeah, the family is throwing a big party for the prodigal son."

"They didn't throw one for you."

"Different situation."

"Because you're not home to stay?"

"Something like that." His gaze slid sideways to Julia, pleating the folds of the sheet in her lap. "Are you coming to the homecoming party?"

"Sure thing. I have to be there to welcome my new deputy sheriff."

"Who'll be minding the store?"

"Zack's got it covered."

That gave Ryder a warm and fuzzy feeling. "Okay, see you there, and keep me updated on Brody."

Ryder ended the call and tossed the phone on the bed. "That's it. Brody's car took a tumble off Highway 160. He died in the crash."

Julia sawed her bottom lip. "That's the same highway I went over."

"It's a dangerous road."

"But I crashed in a snowstorm. It's summer, and we haven't even had a summer drizzle."

"That highway is a hazard any time of the year, especially if you're agitated. You're safe now, babe."

"Yeah, I guess I am."

Ryder scooped her against his chest and stroked her hair. "You're safe."

"Why'd you do it?"

"The LAPD doesn't have enough officers to police that city. The department is understaffed and underappreciated. Time to go." Rafe shrugged and took a long pull from his beer.

Ryder kicked the leg of his little brother's chair. "The truth. It was a woman, wasn't it?"

Rafe studied the label on his bottle and scratched a corner with his fingernail. "Two women."

"Unbelievable. Do Pam and Dad know they owe the presence of their darling boy to a ménage à trois gone bad?"

"Whoa, who said anything about a threesome? I take my women one at a time…on alternate days." Rafe stretched his lanky legs in front of him, crossing his arms behind his head.

"And they had a problem with that? I've seen the women you date."

"Nothing wrong with an air-headed bimbo. Much less work. Why are we talking about my personal life when yours is so much more interesting for a change? I was back in town for five minutes when I heard you and the amnesia chick were an item and I'm an uncle."

Crossing his arms, Ryder bunched his fists against his biceps. Rafe could make light of the women he dated, but he'd better not try that crap with Julia.

"Don't call her that. She's almost completely regained her memory, and yeah, I'm a dad if you can believe that."

"That's a hard one to swallow from the antifamily man." A smile quirked the corner of Rafe's mouth. "But that's one cute little girl…Shelby, not Julia. Don't punch me."

"I didn't realize you were around long enough to meet them."

"I saw them around a few times in the weeks I was here before heading off to the academy."

"They'll be at the party, and I don't want you hitting on Julia or otherwise being an ass." Ryder stood up when he saw Gracie Malone coming up the drive, carrying an apple pie. Charlie followed behind, grasping a crate with two more pies.

Rafe shook his head. "That's cold, dude. I don't hit on my brothers' girlfriends."

"What about Sheila Cramer?"

"High school? You're bringing up high school? I've matured since then." Rafe's boyish grin cracked his face.

"Yeah, right." Ryder jogged down the porch steps and reached for Gracie's pie. "Let me get that for you, Gracie. I'll bring it to Pam in the kitchen."

"She must be bursting at the seams now that she has a grand-daughter." Gracie's nose twitched. "I'm sure that put Millie Stoker's nose out of joint, because she set herself up as Shelby's adoptive grandmother. I always thought that was greedy of her. She has plenty of grandchildren of her own, which is more than some of us can claim."

She shot Charlie a withering look, and he hunched his shoulders, which made him look even more like the Incredible Hulk.

Turning toward the door with the warm pie balanced on his palms, Ryder compressed his lips. *He thought Pam was bad.* He pitied the poor guy.

An hour later, Siverhill's locals filled up the McClintocks' ranch house and spilled onto the patio in the back of the house. Ryder circled his parents' large oak dining room table, which almost groaned beneath the platters and bowls of home-cooked food. In Silverhill they did things old-school. Rafe had some adjustments ahead of him.

Ryder dropped some ribs on his plate, followed by some of Millie's potato salad, and spread some butter on a hot roll straight out of Mrs. Ballard's oven.

While he ate and chatted, he kept one eye on the entrance. Julia and Shelby hadn't shown up yet. Because of all the small-town gossip, he and Julia decided to break the news to Shelby yesterday that she had a father. They'd held their breaths while Shelby wrinkled her small nose. Then she patted Ryder's knee and asked, "Can I call you 'Daddy' now?"

Totally choked him up. Julia had smiled, but a small crease appeared between her brows. She still didn't completely trust him and she was probably wise not to. He didn't know how long he could remain a father to Shelby.

Then he heard a high-pitched giggle and a little whirling dervish with flying golden curls was barreling straight toward him. He caught Shelby in his arms and knew he'd be her father forever.

Tucking her under one arm, he held his hand out to Julia. Her fingers curled around his. "Sorry we're late, but I let Shelby nap longer than usual so she could stay up for the party."

"That's a good excuse, isn't it, Shelby?"

Shelby kicked her legs out behind her and squealed.

"I think it's time I met the happy family." Rafe sauntered up to Julia, his hands shoved into his tight blue jeans, a lazy smile on his face.

Ryder drew his finger across his throat. "Julia, this is my worthless brother, Rafe. Rafe, this is Julia Rousseau and Shelby."

"Worthless? How can he be worthless? He's the new deputy sheriff in town."

"Why, thank you, ma'am." Rafe captured Julia's hand and kissed it. Then he tweaked one of Shelby's curls. "Hey, gorgeous."

Shelby slapped his hand away, and Ryder laughed. "You have the right idea, Shelby. And don't let the badge fool you, Julia. He's bad to the bone."

"Speaking of the badge, is your boss here tonight?" Julia swept her arm around the room.

Ryder shot her a glance. "Why, did you hear anything more about Brody?"

"No, but I thought the San Juan County Coroner's Office was doing a preliminary autopsy today."

Rafe took a break from pinching Shelby's painted toes,

twisting his head over his shoulder. "Autopsy's done. That's why Ballard stayed at the station. He'll be here later."

Ryder hoisted Shelby in his arms. "Let's get this over with and find my parents."

"Nice to meet you, Rafe." Julia waved.

"Don't encourage him."

Ryder circled the group where Pam and his father were holding court, commandeering the conversation as usual. He'd dealt with his dominating parents by leaving, Rafe laughed it off or charmed his way through it and Rod stayed and fought it out with them every day.

He grabbed Julia's and Shelby's hands and took the plunge, and then gritted his teeth while Pam fawned over Shelby. Pam told anyone who would listen about Shelby's riding lessons and how she was a McClintock through and through. He rolled his eyes at Julia, who tilted her head at him.

Standing on tiptoes, she whispered in his ear, "What's wrong?"

He pulled her out of the clump of people hanging on his mother's every word. "Give them ten minutes more and they'll have Shelby's entire future mapped out for her."

"That's what parents do. God knows, my mom tried it with me. I don't know what you're complaining about. If I had a parent who smothered me with attention, maybe I never would've been lost all those years. Maybe someone would've come looking for me." Julia's eyes grew bright.

"I should've come looking for you." He traced a finger along her soft earlobe.

"Why didn't you?"

Ryder blinked. He didn't want to go through this with her again, especially now when he hadn't received orders about his next assignment. "Do you remember we had a…disagreement before I left for Somalia?"

"We had a fight." Her jaw hardened. "And I didn't even know you'd gone off to Somalia. You wouldn't tell me where you were going, remember that?"

"Top secret orders."

"Yeah, I know. That's why I didn't tell you about the pregnancy. I didn't want to force you to change your plans or force you into a commitment you obviously weren't ready to make."

"I understand and I don't blame you for it."

Julia's eyes, soft with tears a moment ago, glittered dangerously. He knew that sign.

"You don't blame me? How thoughtful and caring of you because you're the one who ran away." She drew away from him and folded her arms over her chest. "Are you going to run again?"

Damn. Exactly where he didn't want to go.

"It's called a job. It's not running."

"It's called cowardice." Julia spun around and stalked toward the food-laden table, tears blurring her vision.

She grabbed a chicken leg and tore into it with her teeth. She recalled those discussions all too well. Ryder wanted her in Paris, and after her separation from Jeremy, he got her. They'd reveled in two months of joy and passion and love in a city made for romance.

Then one day he just started making arrangements for his departure. The love she'd nurtured in her heart meant nothing to him. How could he just walk out of her life for two years, correspondence between them screened, blacked out if necessary, and delayed for months?

Now here they were four years later in the same spot, but instead of a pregnancy, she had a four-year-old daughter. And it didn't matter. He still planned to leave them.

Her cell phone buzzed in the pocket of her skirt and she

grabbed a napkin to wipe off her greasy fingers. She plucked the phone from her pocket and flipped it open. A text message.

News on the doc meet me at the end of the drive Z.

Biting her lip, still salty from the chicken, she snapped the phone shut and dropped it back into her pocket where it clicked against her car keys. Did Zack have something on the autopsy report?

She scanned the room for Ryder and spotted him in deep conversation with Rod. As his head dipped toward his brother, the light from a nearby lamp caught the gold highlights in his hair and her fingers itched to comb through it.

She pursed her lips. He didn't deserve to know. Besides, she'd better get used to handling stuff on her own. Pretty soon she wouldn't have Ryder McClintock to run to for comfort anymore.

Pam was still holding Shelby, while she chatted with her friends. Julia shuffled through the crowd.

"Pam, could you please watch Shelby? I'm going out front."

"What?" Pam cupped her ear.

"Could you please keep an eye on Shelby? I'm…"

Pam waved her hand. "You go right ahead."

On her way to the front door, Julia squeezed past Rafe. "Excuse me."

"Anytime, pretty lady."

She rolled her eyes. Did that crap really work in L.A.? She slid through the door and pulled it closed behind her. The buzz from the party filtered into the cool evening, and she inhaled the fresh mountain air and her momentary solitude.

Lights illuminated the McClintocks' drive, but it curved so she couldn't see the gateway at the end. Did Zack park his squad car down there?

Her low heels crunched on the gravel of the drive. Birds twittered and rustled in the thick foliage that ringed the McClintock ranch. Her eyes darted toward a clump of bushes. At least she hoped birds were making those noises and not a skunk.

She glanced backward. She could still hear a hum of voices and see an aura of light, but she could no longer see the house.

Peering into the darkness at the end of the drive, she called out, "Zack?"

Had he parked his car outside the gate? A breeze lifted the edge of her skirt and a chill stole across her flesh. Julia stepped through the gateway. Most of the party guests had parked their cars on the road, but she couldn't see a squad car. Why was it so dark out here?

Her shoe ground into something hard and she looked down. Broken glass littered the dirt. The two lights on either side of the McClintocks' wide gate to their property lay shattered on the ground.

A cold fear gripped the back of her neck and she pivoted on her toes, turning back toward the house.

Too late.

Strong arms pinioned her from behind. She gathered her breath to scream, but a large, gloved hand clamped over her mouth, smashing her lips against her teeth.

One thought thumped in her chest along with the fear: her stalker wasn't dead.

But she might be.

Chapter Eleven

"Another slice of heaven?" Gracie Malone extended a plate under Ryder's nose.

His mouth watered at the scent of warm cinnamon apple pie piled high with vanilla ice cream, but he held out his hands, palms up. "No, thanks, Gracie. I had a piece."

"Just one?" She clicked her tongue. "My Charlie can polish off half a pie."

"Go ahead and give him mine."

"I would, but I don't know where he is." Her brow furrowed.

"Me, please." Shelby had squirmed in between them and now held her hands up toward the pie, wiggling her fingers.

"Isn't she just the cutest little thing?" Gracie chucked Shelby under the chin.

Ryder crouched down on one knee. "Nice manners, Shelby, but you are not having another piece of pie. You already had a piece of pie and two of Millie's homemade cookies. You're done, kiddo."

Gracie beamed. "Well, look at you, acting like a father already. Are you going to make an honest woman of Julia or are you going to take off for some foreign hellhole, like you usually do?"

God, the woman had a big mouth. He grabbed the pie plate and handed it down to Shelby, while he scowled at Gracie.

She continued, oblivious. "Because if you and Julia aren't going to tie the knot, I don't mind telling you that she and Charlie were quite an item last winter—skiing together, sharing hot cocoa by the fire, he even shoveled her driveway."

He opened his mouth to deliver a sarcastic comment, but his cell phone saved him. He put up a finger and dug his phone out of his pocket, checking the display.

"Hey, Sheriff, you got anything on Brody's autopsy?"

"Hello, Ryder. Yeah, that's why I'm calling. I tried Julia's number first, but she didn't answer."

"It's noisy in here."

"I've got some interesting news for you about Brody, interesting and disturbing."

"Disturbing?" Ryder's pulse thrummed in his throat.

"Seems Dr. Brody was intoxicated at the time of the car accident. Way over the legal limit."

"So? He still could've climbed that trail and dumped the boulder on Julia. Maybe he got drunk later."

"That's just it, Ryder. There was no later."

"Damn it, Ballard. Spit it out." Ryder's heart hammered in his chest and he took a swig of his beer to moisten his dry mouth.

"Dr. Brody's car went off the road on Tuesday night. He couldn't have pushed that rock over the cliff. He was already dead."

Ryder clicked his phone shut, the blood roaring in his ears. His gaze swept back and forth across the room. He hadn't seen Julia for the past ten minutes.

"Something wrong, Ryder?" Gracie's beady eyes studied his face.

"Have you seen Julia?"

"Not lately. Why?"

He dropped to his knees in front of Shelby and dabbed a drop of ice cream from her nose. "Where's Mommy?"

She hunched her shoulders. "She told me to stay with Gamma Pam, but you had pie."

Shoving up from the floor, he put his hand on Shelby's back. "Let's go back to…Gamma Pam."

He tapped his stepmother on the shoulder and she swung around.

"There you are and with another piece of pie. I can see your daddy's going to be a pushover…."

"Pam," he interrupted her. "Have you seen Julia?"

"Not since she dropped Shelby off with me and asked me to watch her."

"Where did she go?"

"I don't know. I didn't hear her above this noise, especially with that music blaring outside."

"Watch Shelby again and this time keep her with you." He pushed through the crowd and stumbled out to the patio in the back.

A younger group mingled out here, drinking beer and listening to hip-hop. He spied Rafe, sitting on the deck's railing, with his legs hooked around the new waitress from the Main Street Café.

"Have you seen Julia?"

Rafe's ready grin faded. "About ten minutes ago. What's wrong?"

"Where'd you see her?"

"She was eating at the table and then she went outside."

"Outside the front door?" Ryder could barely squeeze the words past his tight throat.

"Yeah. She left about ten minutes ago." Rafe repeated, "What's wrong?"

But Ryder was already charging through the house toward the front door. He slammed it behind him and ran down the drive. "Julia?"

A few guests had driven their cars up the drive and parked in the circular driveway that fronted the house, but usually people parked on the street. He didn't see Julia's car, and she arrived too late to get a spot close to the house. Maybe she just went back to her car outside the gate.

Ryder rounded the last bend of the drive and froze. Complete darkness shrouded the end of the driveway at the gates where floodlights usually illuminated the entryway. He shouted, "Julia?"

He charged into the black night, adrenaline coursing through his body, all his instincts on high alert. He sensed the struggle in the row of cars to his right before he saw or heard anything.

Then a sob and a hiss disturbed the silence. Didn't sound like two lovers. He spun around to confront the sounds. The strident blare of a car alarm pierced the night. In the flashing headlights, two figures peeled apart and one dark form plunged away from the car and shot across the road.

A woman screamed, almost drowning out the car alarm. Julia! The headlights outlined Julia, staggering to her feet.

He rushed to her side and she collapsed against his chest, sobbing. "H-he tried…"

"Shh. You're safe now." Hadn't he just told her that two nights ago? "I suppose you didn't get a good look at him?"

Releasing a shuddering breath, she whispered, "He had a ski mask on. I felt it on his face as we struggled." She squirmed out of his arms and pointed across the road. "He took off that way. You have to catch him."

"I'm not leaving you alone." He smoothed his hands down her trembling back.

"Then stay here. I'll go after him." Rafe stepped from the shadows, his gun drawn.

Julia gestured toward the dense bushes. "He ran in there."

"You'll never find anything in this darkness and by the time I run back to the house to get a flashlight, he'll be long gone."

"I have this." Rafe dangled his keychain, which had a small flashlight attached to it. "He's probably long gone already, but if he dropped something or snagged something on a twig maybe I'll find it before he has time to come back and retrieve it."

As Rafe crossed the street and crashed through the foliage, Ryder pulled Julia back into his arms. "Are you all right? Did he hurt you?"

"No." She shivered, and he rubbed her bare arms. "He tried to kidnap me, Ryder. If he'd had a weapon, a knife or even a rope, he could've killed me. Instead, he tried to abduct me. When you arrived, he was fumbling for something in his pocket. I smelled alcohol or ether."

His chest tightened. God, he almost lost her. Again.

She stifled a sob. "He was going to knock me out. When I heard your voice, I kicked out my legs at that car's bumper, which set off the alarm. If you hadn't come along…"

"But I did." He rested his chin on top of her head and stroked her hair. "When I couldn't find you at the house, I panicked."

She lifted her head. "Why? We both thought Dr. Brody was the stalker and he's dead."

"While I was at the party, Sheriff Ballard called with the autopsy report. He told me Brody's car went off the cliff the night before the attack on you. Brody couldn't have been responsible for that."

"But you found the card case with his cards."

"Did Brody ever visit you here?"

"We had a couple of sessions at my house, and I took him on a hike once up to The Twirling Ballerinas, but that was over a year ago. The case you showed me hadn't been lying in the dirt, exposed to the elements for a year."

"Someone planted the case to set him up." He massaged Julia's knotted shoulders. Keeping her talking seemed to calm her down. Better to concentrate on logic right now than emotion.

"Where would someone get a hold of Dr. Brody's cards?"

"A patient." Why didn't he think of that before? "Did you ever talk to any of Brody's other patients? Does he work with any seriously disturbed people?"

She shook her head. "I usually left his office before the next patient showed up, and Dr. Brody never discussed his patients with me."

"His behavior was hardly ethical. It wouldn't surprise me." Ryder choked back the rest of his words. Julia didn't need him to remind her that she'd trusted the wrong guy…again.

He lifted a shoulder. "Whoever planted the case did it to lull us into a false sense of security. You never would've come out here on your own if you thought your stalker was still at large. Why *did* you come out here?"

Her hand flew to her mouth. "My cell phone. I got a text message from Zack telling me to meet him out here for information about Brody."

Ryder snapped his fingers. "That message can be traced, but first I'm taking you back to the party."

"Wait." She pulled back from him and dug her feet into the ground. "I don't want you to charge into the party and make some big announcement about this. We'll tell Sheriff Ballard but no one else."

"What if somebody saw this guy or something unusual before the party started?"

"Ballard can question them later. This is a small town. It's all going to come out anyway, but I don't want to slink back into that party with victim written all over me. I'm done with that role."

Someone darted across the road. Julia jumped and Ryder shoved her behind his body.

A small light played across the ground and Rafe shouted, "It's me."

"Did you find anything?"

"Too damn dark. I'll do a search tomorrow morning." Rafe shook some leaves and twigs from his hair. "Can you describe anything about this guy, Julia? Height? Build? Smell? Did he say anything to you?"

"Let's take this conversation into the light." Putting his hand on Julia's back, Ryder propelled her back up the drive under the lights.

"It was so dark and he came at me from behind. He was tall and strong. He didn't say one word. The only smell I could detect was the ether, and it scared the sh…" A furrow formed between her brows.

"What's wrong?" Ryder grabbed her cold hands and chaffed them.

"He pinned me against his body with one arm while he was getting the ether ready, and for one second before the smell of the ether invaded my nose, I smelled…cologne."

"Did you recognize the cologne?"

Ryder flashed his brother an admiring look. Rafe definitely had the instincts of a cop.

"It smelled familiar, but I can't place it. I probably just smelled it in a department store or something. Not many men around Silverhill wear cologne."

"Except Zack Ballard." Ryder crossed his arms over his chest. "And he's the one who sent you the message to meet him."

"That's crazy. He wouldn't text me on my cell if he planned to kidnap me."

"He figured after he abducted you, he'd have your phone anyway." He was grasping at straws here, but he wanted to pin this on somebody.

"Slow down, bro." Rafe pulled his cell phone out of his pocket. "There's one way to find out if Zack is the one who left the message for Julia. I have his cell phone number right here."

Julia dragged her cell out of her pocket and flipped it open. She squinted at the display and read off the number that sent her the text message.

Rafe whistled. "Zack's dumber than he looks. He sent Julia that message from his own cell phone. I'm going to give him a call back."

Rafe pressed a few buttons on his cell phone and then shook his head. "Not answering, which doesn't surprise me."

"I can't believe it." Julia stepped back and stumbled. "I know Zack. He can't be responsible."

Ryder reached out and Julia knocked his hand away. First Dr. Brody and now Zack. The thought that her stalker might be someone she knew and trusted bothered her. She'd loved and trusted her father so much and when he died she thought she'd never find a man with those qualities. But Jeremy tricked her into believing she had and now she'd fallen into the same trap with Dr. Brody and Zack...and him?

"Let's call Sheriff Ballard." Rafe got on his cell and reached Ballard on his way to the party. He told him about the attack on Julia and how the stalker lured her out of the house. "It looks like Zack might be involved, Sheriff."

Five minutes later, Ballard's squad car roared to a stop in

front of the McClintocks' gateway and he barreled out of the car, leaving the door open.

"You okay, honey?" He patted Julia on the shoulder. "Damn, I thought we had our man. Now let me see this message."

Julia showed him the text message on her phone and Ballard swore.

"I know my boy's not the sharpest tool in the shed, but he doesn't have an aggressive bone in his body. That's why he pumps all that iron…it's all about the look."

"When was the last time you spoke to Zack?" Ryder had to agree with Ballard. Zack presented an imposing figure, but he shied away from using force. But maybe that's why he attacked women.

"I talked to him on the radio about two hours ago. He was on his way to investigate a report of a transient living in the caves by The Twirling Ballerinas."

Rafe asked, "Have you tried him on the radio since then?"

"On the way over here after I got your call. He didn't respond."

Ballard's radio crackled from the squad car as if on cue, and all three of them spun around and stared at the car.

"This might be him now." Ballard trod back to his car, dropped onto the seat and grabbed the radio.

Ryder exchanged a glance with Rafe. Yeah, now that he made his attack on Julia?

The voice of Racine Elder, the dispatcher, hissed and popped over the radio. "Sheriff, we got a call about a squad car parked at the end of Main Street. It's been there for two hours and it looks like it's Zack's car. Over."

"Ten-four, Racine. I'll check it out. Over." Ballard leaned on his car door and winked. "Maybe Zack's just spending some time with that little gal he's been seeing, the new girl at Gracie's B and B."

Julia let out a long breath. "You see, it couldn't have been Zack. There's no way he could've come out here on foot, and his car's been parked on Main for the past two hours."

"Unless he took another mode of transportation," murmured Rafe. "Wait up, Sheriff. I'm coming with you."

"I'm following. It's time to get this straightened out." Ryder turned to Julia. "I'll walk you back up to the house."

"Oh no, you don't. If this is a caravan, then I'm tagging along. If Zack did text me, I'm going to find out what the hell he wanted. Just give me a minute to look in on Shelby."

"She's with my stepmother. She'll be fine. Do you have your car keys? I can't pull my truck out of the drive with all these cars parked here."

She dangled the keys in front of his nose and he snatched them from her. "I'll drive."

Rafe joined Ballard in the squad car, which Ryder followed as it pulled into the road. Julia sat beside him with her hands clasped between her knees. He knew she wanted Zack's name cleared, but a sense of dread hammered against his brain. If Zack wasn't her stalker, who was?

Ballard's car pulled up behind the squad car parked at the foot of the Ballerina Trail. Rafe exited the car, leaving Ballard behind.

"What's going on?" Ryder jogged up to his brother while Julia scrambled out of the car after him.

"This doesn't feel right to me, Ryder. I told Ballard to wait in the car. He's too personally involved." Rafe drew his gun.

"What's he going to do, shoot Zack?" Julia scowled.

"You," Ryder took her arm, "wait by the car with Sheriff Ballard."

Ryder crept up to Zack's squad car next to Rafe. Rafe opened the car door and the dome light illuminated the interior.

A set of keys dangled in the ignition and the radio crackled with static. No Zack.

While Rafe inspected the car, Ryder grabbed the flash-light Rafe had taken from Ballard and beamed the light across the ground at the foot of the trail. It tripped over an object in the bushes.

Ryder edged forward and shone the light on the object stuck in a bush. Zack's hat.

Gripping the flashlight, Ryder made his way a few feet up the trail and stopped cold.

Zack Ballard was blocking the trail.

And he was dead.

Chapter Twelve

Julia held Sheriff Ballard's big, rough hand in hers, as he wiped his arm across his face.

"It's my fault. The boy wasn't cut out for police work and I pushed him into it."

"Shh." She squeezed his hand. "Zack loved his job and he was good at it. He was perfect as a small-town sheriff. Who knew a killer would come to Silverhill?"

A killer after her.

Sheriff Ballard pushed off the car and hunched his shoulders. "I suppose I have to go home now and tell his mother."

"Give her my love and let me know if the two of you need anything." Julia wiped a tear from her face as she watched Sheriff Ballard plod back to his car.

Ryder and Rafe approached her with the sheriff from San Juan County. Ryder said, "Julia, Sheriff Vickers wants to have a look at your cell phone and that message from Zack."

She pulled out the phone and handed it to Sheriff Vickers. "What about Zack's phone? Does the message show on his phone, too?"

Ryder blew out a breath. "Zack's phone is missing along with his gun."

"So whoever shot Zack took his cell phone and used it to leave me that text message?" Julia hugged herself and ground her teeth together to stop their chattering.

"That's what it looks like, Ms. Rousseau. I'm going to use that phone message to work out a time line." Sheriff Vickers peered at the display on her phone and jotted down some notes in his spiral.

"Deputy Sheriff Ballard took a radio call about a transient up at The Twirling Ballerinas at eight twenty-three p.m. Someone sent this text message to your phone at eight forty-one p.m. So we can pinpoint the time of death in those twenty minutes, unless Deputy Sheriff Ballard sent the message himself while he was still alive."

"I don't think that's probable." Rafe scratched his chin and jerked his thumb toward the trail. "Are your men investigating this transient? With Zack's gun missing, it's likely the shooter used it to kill him."

Sheriff Vickers snapped his notebook shut. "We'll know that for sure when ballistics gets that bullet out of Ballard's head. My men are searching the trail now. So far, nothing."

"Your men don't know that trail and they don't know the caves at the top of the trail. This is your investigation now, but I'm going to search the trail and caves tomorrow." Rafe planted his legs apart and shoved his hands in his pockets.

"Knock yourself out, but anything you find comes to us."

As the San Juan County Sheriff and crime scene personnel packed up to leave, Ryder and Rafe watched through identical narrowed eyes.

These McClintocks knew how to take charge.

"What now?" Julia had already called Ryder's stepmother, and Shelby was sound asleep. Thank God Mrs. Ballard had left the party early because her husband had to work late, sparing

Julia any questions. By now Sheriff Ballard had probably delivered the crushing news. Julia's lip quivered and another tear hung on her lashes.

Ryder drew her close and caught her tear on the end of his thumb. "You're not going back home. You're staying with us tonight and every other night until we find this maniac."

"Do you think he killed Zack because Zack discovered him in the caves or do you think the transient is someone different altogether and Zack just bumbled into the path of the stalker?" Julia couldn't even voice her other worry, that the killer lured Zack to this spot to kill him and take his phone to text her or to set up Zack.

Just like he set up Dr. Brody.

"Ryder." She clutched his arm. "Do you think this guy had anything to do with Dr. Brody's accident? It's the same pattern. He sets someone up as the stalker and then kills him."

"I just don't know, Julia. There are too many questions, but if I ever get my hands on this son of a…" Ryder clenched his fists and banged the roof of her car.

While Ryder and Rafe discussed bullets and guns and trajectories on the way back to the McClintock ranch, Julia sat silently niggling her lower lip.

Her stalker was a murderer, but when he had her in his clutches tonight he didn't kill her even though he could have. Did he intend to kill her on the trail or just wound her so he could drag her away?

What did he want with her?

JULIA PLAYED with her scrambled eggs as the third McClintock argument of the morning erupted in the kitchen.

"You're not turning any part of the McClintock ranch into a dude ranch." Ryder's father, Ralph, nearly spat out the offensive words.

"I'm not discussing this anymore. I have to go out and make sure that irrigation system gets repaired, so we can feed the cattle, or otherwise, I'm turning the whole damn ranch into a dude ranch." Rod slammed out the front door.

"Home sweet home." Ryder ducked behind his newspaper.

Pam joined them at the dining room table and poured herself another cup of coffee. "Your father and Rod have been having this argument for a year. Rod wants to start giving riding lessons to attract the summer crowd and Ralph won't hear of it."

"It's expensive to run a working ranch these days." Ryder lifted a shoulder. "Does Pop want Rod to stay and manage the ranch or not? If so, he'd better start listening to him."

"Maybe if there were two of you working on Ralph, he'd come around." She raised her eyebrows at Ryder, but he burrowed deeper into his newspaper.

"You have a family now, a daughter. How are you going to raise a daughter when you're off on another assignment somewhere? And Rafe, first week on the job and there's a cop killer roaming the streets of Silverhill."

Now Julia felt like burrowing into a newspaper.

Ryder smacked down his paper. "Pam, that's between Julia and me. It's none of your business. I thought you had cooking to do for Mrs. Ballard."

"I do." Pam sighed as she pushed up from the table. "Terrible tragedy. Do they really think the man who killed Zack is the same man who's been bothering Julia?"

Now Julia felt like crawling under the table.

"Yeah, we do, and he's been doing more than bothering Julia. He attacked her two nights ago outside the ranch."

She wrinkled her brow. "Yes, trouble sure does seem to follow you around, Julia."

"Pam."

"I'm just saying." Pam raised her hands. "Do you think Shelby would like to help me in the kitchen when she wakes up? When does she wake up? It's getting awfully late."

Julia shot Ryder a warning look. She couldn't handle another McClintock argument this morning. She smiled at Pam. "I'm sure she'd like that."

LATER THAT AFTERNOON after Shelby's riding lesson, Julia sat on the porch swing while Ryder perched on the top step.

"I'm sorry we got into it at the party, Julia. Is that why you went off to meet Zack by yourself instead of coming to get me?"

"If you're not going to be around, Shelby and I better not count on you." She put the swing into motion and folded a leg beneath her.

"You and Shelby can always count on me."

"Little hard to do when you're hiding out in a cave somewhere." She had no intention of begging him to stay. She didn't do it in Paris and she wouldn't do it here.

"I don't know where I'm going yet."

"How exciting for you." She gave a typically Parisian lift of the shoulders. "I'm thinking about going to Paris at the end of the summer to visit my mother anyway. Then I'll decide if I want to continue working toward my psychology degree and whether or not I want to stay in Silverhill."

His eyebrows shot up. "You'd leave Silverhill?"

"The place creeps me out." She used to feel safe and protected in Silverhill, ringed in by the Rockies and surrounded by good people. Now nothing was as it seemed, and with her memory back, she no longer felt the need to hide from the rest of the world. She had a place in it and she'd already taken the first step to end the estrangement between her and her mother.

Ryder pushed off the step and collapsed next to her in the swing, rocking it back and forth. His tight jaw and narrowed eyes meant business, but what would he get out of it if she stayed in Silverhill? He wouldn't be here to boss her around anyway.

Rafe's squad car emerged from a cloud of dust on the gravel drive, saving Julia from this particular discussion with Ryder. He squealed to a stop on the circular driveway in front of the house and slid from the car, twirling his cowboy hat on his hand. The sun glinted off his shiny badge.

"I'm glad to find the two of you together, not that that's hard to do these days." He flashed a dimpled smile. "I have more news from Brody's preliminary autopsy."

Julia held her breath. She couldn't take any more bad news. Despite her earlier resolve to be independent of Ryder's comfort, she slid her hand onto his thigh.

"Whaddya got?" Ryder curled his fingers around hers, his previous intensity gone.

"The man was drunk as a skunk. His blood alcohol level was twice the legal limit. So even if someone hadn't given him a little shove down the embankment, he was headed for trouble on that stretch of the road."

"Someone pushed his car off the road?" Julia knew that stretch of the road too well. She shivered and convulsively clutched Ryder's hand. First Brody, then Zack.

Nodding, Rafe sank to the top step, stretching out his long legs. "His back bumper was dented, and a car left a blue streak on his paint. Brody went over that cliff nose first. All the damage from the impact occurred on the front of the car."

"Any leads or witnesses?" Ryder squeezed Julia's hand right back.

"The night of the accident, the bartender and a few patrons at the Silver Rim Lounge in Durango reported that Brody was boozing it up at the bar. Another man joined him and kept buying him drinks and they stumbled out of the bar together at closing time."

A furrow formed between Ryder's brows. "Was Brody a drinker?"

"He was an alcoholic in recovery. That's how he got into hypnosis. It helped him stop drinking." Julia tilted her chin, defying Ryder to comment on the impropriety of a therapist discussing his personal life with a client. She'd been a fool not to have seen Dr. Brody's growing attraction to her, but she didn't need Ryder's judgment.

But condemnation of her relationship with Dr. Brody appeared to be the last thing on Ryder's mind, as he absently rubbed his thumb along her wrist. "Did any of the witnesses in the bar give you a description of the man?"

"Sure did. Dark, curly hair, sunglasses and covered up."

"Covered up?" Julia quirked a brow at Rafe. "What does that mean?"

"The guy was overdressed for the weather outside and the temperature in the bar. In addition to jeans, he was wearing a long-sleeve turtleneck and had a knit cap pulled low on his forehead."

"How did the witnesses notice his hair then?" Ryder asked.

"It was sticking out beneath the edge of the cap."

"Whoa." Julia held up her hands. "Back up a minute. The guy was wearing sunglasses indoors?"

Rafe shrugged. "Happens all the time in L.A. Jack Nicholson always wears sunglasses."

"We're not in L.A. and I'm sure that wasn't Jack Nicholson." Julia clamped a hand over her mouth. Sunglasses at night. The man in the blue car who tried to get her to pull over.

"What's wrong, babe?"

Julia jumped from the swing and clasped the swing's chain

for support. "I've seen that man. Ryder, I told you about him after the break-in at my house."

Ryder and Rafe both shot to their feet and peppered her with questions. She told Rafe about driving home from her last class of the semester and the man in the dark blue sedan who tried to get her pull over for a flat tire that didn't exist.

"Did you see him again?" Rafe pulled a notebook from his pocket and flipped it open. "Did you get a license plate number?"

She shook her head. "I never saw him again, but then I didn't get a good look at him. I just remember the sunglasses. Do you think he's the monster who's been stalking me? Do you think he drove Dr. Brody off the road and killed Zack?"

A wave of nausea washed over her and she clutched her stomach, doubling over. If she had pulled over that night she might already be dead. No, not dead. He didn't want to kill her. He made that clear the other night.

Ryder's strong arms led her back to the porch swing and he sat next to her, holding her close. "At least he's out in the open now. People have seen him. You've seen him."

"Not really." She wiped the back of her hand across her clammy brow. "I probably wouldn't recognize him if I ran into him on Main Street. The sunglasses, the hat, the clothes. He's wearing a disguise, isn't he?"

"Maybe." Rafe leaned against the porch railing and shoved his notebook back in his pocket. "But it's more than you had before."

"Do you have a composite drawing of the man in the bar with Brody?"

"Not yet, but we're working on it."

"How are Sheriff Ballard and his wife holding up?" Julia rested her head on Ryder's shoulder. Might as well take advantage of his presence in Silverhill while it lasted. Who knew how long he planned to stay? Maybe he'd leave before the police even caught this guy.

Rafe lifted a shoulder. "The sheriff's a stoic old guy, but Mrs. Ballard is wrecked. She's been wanting to move nearer to her daughter's family in Atlanta, and I think this is going to be the deciding factor. She can't stay here."

Julia knew the feeling. Some maniac had shattered their peaceful existence in Silverhill and she brought him here. Her neighbors, who had once welcomed her, now eyed her with suspicion and thinly veiled hostility. She recognized the looks. The people of Silverhill had directed the same looks her way when the media descended on the town, bringing with them a circus atmosphere in their zeal to cover Julia's bizarre story.

She got the looks again when the good folks of Silverhill discovered she'd had a relationship and a child with one of its own eligible bachelors.

Even Ryder's stepmother alluded to Julia's disruptive effect on the town of Silverhill. Perhaps it was time to wrap up this chapter of her life and move back to Paris. She'd already written a letter to her mother, sending pictures of Shelby. If her mother wanted to see her, she'd hop on the next flight to the city of lights and romance…as a single mom.

Charlie Malone's jeep crawled up the drive and he pulled to a stop in front of the house. He lumbered up the walkway and nodded to the two McClintock brothers, ignoring Rafe's outstretched hand. "My mom sent me over to pick up some food for the Ballards."

"Is your mom over there now?" Julia asked.

Charlie nodded. "Mrs. Ballard is going back to Atlanta with her daughter, Kelly, after Zack's funeral."

Julia rose from the swing and took Charlie's hand, squeezing it. "I'm sorry. I know Zack was your friend."

"Didn't the two of you have a fight last week?" Rafe slid his back up the post and crossed his arms. "Sheriff Ballard said he caught the two of you arguing about something at the B and B."

"It wasn't a fight." Charlie puffed out his chest and glared at Rafe.

"Whatever it was, you owe me an explanation. Like it or not, I'm the new Deputy Sheriff in town."

Rafe hadn't moved a muscle and he still slumped against the post, but his glittering blue eyes signaled danger.

Charlie read the sign loud and clear. He coughed. "We had a…discussion about Rosie."

"Rosie?" Rafe lifted a brow that disappeared beneath the rim of his black cowboy hat.

"She works for us at the B and B." Charlie kicked his boot against the top step. "Me and her are dating, and Zack started to move in on her. When I told him to back off, he laughed at me."

Rafe's eyes narrowed. "So tell me, Charlie, did you decide to get rid of the competition?"

"Rafe!" Julia's voice cracked. Were these McClintocks crazy?

"No." Charlie shoved his hands in his pockets. "I didn't want Zack dead. I just wanted him to leave Rosie alone. And that goes for everyone else. Does your stepmom have that food, Ryder?"

Ryder snapped his gaping mouth shut and shook his head. "She's still cooking. She'll have something later this afternoon and she'll bring it over herself."

Charlie grunted and stomped back to his jeep, little tufts of dust rising from his boots.

Julia blinked. "What was that all about?"

"I think that's Charlie Malone in love." Ryder scratched his chin. "But why does he have it in for you, Rafe?"

Julia said, "Rosie told me right in front of Charlie that she wanted to get to know you better, Rafe. I think Charlie's relationship with Rosie is all in his head, wishful thinking."

Ryder raised one eyebrow. "Have you been hitting on this Rosie chick?"

"I don't think so." Rafe's slow smile claimed his face. "Not that I know of."

"See what I mean, Julia? My brother's nothing but trouble."

"Hold on a minute." She waved her hands in the air as if to disperse the clouds of confusion. "Do you really think Charlie had anything to do with Zack's death?"

Rafe shrugged. "I don't know. Just thought I should stick it to him while the time was right. He was obviously pissed off at me. I wanted to catch him off guard."

"And did you get the response you wanted?" Julia hugged herself, sucking in her bottom lip.

"It's a start." Rafe jerked his head in her direction. "Why, did you catch something?"

"Yeah, a whiff of Charlie's cologne."

TWO DAYS LATER, Ryder kicked his heels up on Rod's desk and placed a call to Black Cobra headquarters in Washington. His supervisor, Jeff Lawrence, had left him a message earlier that morning, and Ryder figured he was calling about the CD. Too early for his next assignment. He had at least another month of leave coming. Maybe he could take Julia and Shelby to his place in South Carolina. And then what?

Ryder left his own message with Jeff's secretary and then tipped his head back on Rod's leather chair. He didn't want to leave until the police caught Julia's stalker…Zack's killer. Did he want to leave at all? He knew with bone-chilling certainty that if he left, he'd be walking out of Julia's and Shelby's lives forever. Julia would never forgive him. And he'd have a helluva time forgiving himself.

Since he'd graduated from dropping bouquets of flowers on her porch, Julia's stalker had been leaving a lot more clues. He'd make a mistake one of these days.

Rafe decided to look at Charlie more closely after his jealous outburst the other day and discovered he didn't have an alibi at the time of Zack's murder. Ryder could imagine Charlie skulking around Julia's house and even slashing his tires, but murder?

The phone rang and he grabbed it before anyone else in the household could get to it. Jeff's voice hissed over the phone. "Are you alone, Ryder?"

"Yep. Did you look at the CD?"

"We got into it. Old news. Of course we don't want it floating around, but the information on that disc isn't going to do our enemies any good now."

Ryder rolled his shoulders, easing the tension out of his muscles. Good news on that front anyway. "That's good to hear. I take it the CD would've caused a lot of damage at the time Jeremy Scott took it."

"A helluva lot of damage. That's why we tried to get it back by any means necessary."

"Any means necessary?" Ryder's heart thudded in his chest. "What are you telling me, Jeff?"

Jeff paused and then his voice came back, smooth as aged cognac. "I'm not telling you anything. As far as we know, the enemy murdered Jeremy Scott, blew him and his house in Tucson sky-high. He probably wouldn't give them the CD. Demanded more money or something. Jeremy was a greedy SOB."

Ryder swallowed and a pain sliced behind his eyes. Did Black Cobra take out one of its agents? He massaged his temples. Ex-agent. Did it really shock him? Black Cobra didn't operate the same way as the CIA. It followed its own rules, its own code of ethics. But those rules could've resulted in Julia's death, too. Did the agency even care if anyone else was in that house?

"Ryder?" Jeff's voice sharpened. "Are you still there?"

"Yeah."

"We won't discuss Jeremy Scott again. You won't discuss him with anyone else."

Did that include Jeremy's ex-wife? "I hear you."

Jeff let out a sigh. "You're leaving for your next assignment in two weeks. Jakarta. You're an arms dealer."

Jeff's words slammed against Ryder's chest, and he almost tipped over in Rod's chair. "Two weeks? What happened to my long leave?"

"I thought you wanted to stay out in the field. You transferred right from Somalia to Chechnya without blinking an eye."

That's because he couldn't find Julia after Somalia. He didn't have any reason to come back to the States and a desk assignment. And now?

"Are you in?" Jeff's voice pressed like a heavy weight against his heart.

If he left for Jakarta in two weeks, he wouldn't be able to protect Julia anymore. Had he really been protecting her? What if he stayed and failed…again?

Ryder dragged in a deep breath. "I'll let you know."

Promising to discuss the issue later, Ryder ended the call and squeezed his eyes shut, pinching the bridge of his nose. Could he stay and make a family with Julia and Shelby? That little girl already had him wrapped around her grubby fingers, but the thought of hearth and home scared the hell out of him.

The phone rang again and when nobody else answered it, he scooped it up and pressed the talk button.

"Hello?"

A woman's husky voice purred over the line. "Can I speak to Ryder McClintock?"

"You're speaking to him."

"When you got back to town, I was hoping I'd get a chance to talk to you, but this isn't what I had in mind." The woman had a throaty growl that promised long nights of sensual pleasures for some lucky guy.

"Who is this?"

"My name's Rosie Fletcher. I work at the Mountain View B and B."

Great. That's all they needed, to get Charlie riled up at another McClintock. "What can I do for you?"

"Oh, it's not what you can do for me, but what I can do for you."

He doubted any woman besides Julia Rousseau could do anything for him. He cleared his throat. "Cut to the chase, Rosie."

"I think I have some information about that accident on Highway 160, the one involving your girlfriend's shrink."

Ryder's pulse quickened. "I'd be interested in hearing about it, but I think you have the wrong McClintock brother. You want my brother, Rafe. He's the lawman."

"You're right. I do want your brother." She gave a low laugh. "But not right now. The information I have is for sale and the last time I checked, the police weren't paying."

"And if I call the sheriff and tell him you have this information?"

"I'll forget it in a hurry."

"How much?"

"Two or three grand. Whatever you have lying around that big, sprawling ranch of yours."

He didn't bother to correct her. The ranch didn't belong to him, but he could lay his hands on a few thousand. "Can you tell me what you have over the phone?"

"Can you lay some cold, hard cash on me over the phone?" She paused as his silence gave her the obvious answer. "I didn't think so. Meet me at guesthouse behind the B and B. You know it? Down by the creek."

"I know where it is."

Ryder agreed to meet Rosie forty-five minutes later. After raiding Rod's safe and stuffing two thousand, three hundred and forty-eight dollars in a manila envelope, Ryder slammed out of the house and hopped in his truck. He'd get the info from Rosie first. If he deemed it of any value, he'd hand over the cash. Then he'd deliver Rosie's information to Rafe.

The Malones' B and B had a guesthouse behind the main house that sat at the edge of a creek. Sometimes Gracie rented it out, especially during ski season, and sometimes she used it to house the seasonal help. Maybe Charlie talked his mother into making it available for Rosie, so he could pay her some private visits away from his mother's watchful gaze.

Ryder parked his truck across the road from the B and B and walked along the side of the property, his boots crunching the gravel. He knew Gracie was with Mrs. Ballard to help her prepare for Zack's funeral tomorrow. He just hoped Charlie had better things to do than spy on Rosie. Ryder didn't need a confrontation with Charlie right now.

Clutching the manila envelope with the cash against his body, Ryder knocked on the door of the guesthouse. No answer. "Rosie?"

He followed the sound of the gurgling stream in back of the guesthouse. The trees across the water swayed in the light breeze, their leaves playing peekaboo with the sun and throwing a dappled pattern on the ground.

A twig snapped and the hair on the back his neck rose. He

narrowed his eyes as he peered into the dense foliage across the creek bed. "Rosie?"

Clambering over a few rocks, Ryder made his way along the edge of the stream and pulled up sharply. A woman crouched over the edge of the water as if drinking from the stream.

With his mouth dry, Ryder crunched through the rocks on the creek bed to reach her side. The woman was kneeling over, face down in the water, her long brown hair fanning out around her.

Ryder swallowed a lump in his throat as he crouched next to her. He nudged one bare shoulder, and a woman he presumed to be Rosie Fletcher fell over on her side. Ryder swore as Rosie's lifeless, bulging eyes stared at him.

At first he thought someone drowned her, but the angry red marks around her throat told a different story. Someone had strangled her and then shoved her head in the water.

Ryder scanned the ground around her body and caught sight of a small, white card floating on the water, caught by a pile of pebbles. He pinched the edge of the card between two fingers and retrieved it from the creek.

Drops of water magnified and distorted the gold embossed letters announcing Dr. Brody's practice. Ryder flicked the soggy card with his index finger, sending pinpoints of water flying into the air. Is this the information Rosie had to offer him? If so, where did she get the card?

He glanced down at Rosie's inert form, the marks on her neck already purpling. Wherever she got the card, that information was lost to him now, sealed behind a dead woman's vacant eyes.

Chapter Thirteen

"For one crazy heart-stopping minute, I thought she was you."

Julia wrapped her hands around a cup of hot tea, trying to warm the chill that invaded her skin. The sun shone brightly in the blue sky, but the news of a third murder blotted out its warmth. A third murder at her door.

"Did the sheriffs find anything on Rosie's body?" Julia lowered her voice as the waitress hovered at the next booth. "Any clue to what information she had about Dr. Brody's accident?"

"Dr. Brody's card was floating in the creek near Rosie's body. I gave it to the cops. It was the least I could do. They're not too happy with me for not calling them first after Rosie told me she had info. I explained that she threatened to clam up if I called the cops, and I didn't even tell them about the money. Except Rafe. I told Rafe."

"Dr. Brody's card?" Julia knitted her brows as she blew on her tea. "His business card? The same as the ones you found on the trail?"

"Exactly the same. Maybe someone had one of those cards, and if that someone wasn't a patient of Brody, it got Rosie thinking about why he had his card."

"They still haven't located Charlie?"

"No, and they're mighty interested in talking to him. Do you want anything to eat along with that tea?"

She shook her head. Ryder had hurried over to the store from the crime scene to tell her about Rosie's murder before she heard it through the grapevine and then dragged her off to Miner's Café for a lunch she didn't feel like eating.

"This is such a mess." Julia covered her face with her hands. "Why would Charlie go through all this trouble to get to me if he wanted Rosie?"

"Maybe he used Rosie as a substitute for you. Maybe he figured once I came back into the picture, he didn't have a chance with you."

She ignored his implication, served with a heaping side of ego. "Don't you have a hard time believing Charlie murdered anyone?"

"People act irrationally. If he's innocent, where is he?"

Her hand jerked, sloshing tea into the saucer, as a horrible thought slammed into her brain. "What if Charlie's dead, too?"

Ryder grasped her hand, droplets of tea and all. "He's not dead. Whether he did it or not, he's running scared. Our guy's not too shy about leaving dead bodies lying around. If he killed Charlie, he wouldn't hide the body. It's as if he's flaunting his cleverness in front of us, like he's playing a game."

Julia shivered and sipped her tea. "I don't think murder is clever."

Ryder thanked the waitress for his burger and fries and dug his elbows into the table on either side of his plate. "He's clever because he's making us suspect our own. What if your stalker is an outsider? This guy with the sunglasses? Or someone staying at one of the B and Bs?"

"Are the police questioning all the guests at the Mountain View?"

"Yeah, but it's Charlie they really want." Ryder squeezed the ketchup bottle, squirting ketchup all over his fries.

"Shelby must've inherited her love of ketchup from you." Julia wrinkled her nose. "She smothers her fries with the stuff, too."

Beaming, Ryder glanced up from his ketchup operation. "She does?"

A pain twisted in her chest. Ryder didn't know much about his daughter. Did he want to learn? Julia flattened her palms on the smooth tabletop. "Was Gracie there?"

"Nope."

"She's about to get a taste of her own busybody medicine." She grimaced, the thought giving her no satisfaction at all.

Ryder popped a drenched french fry into his mouth and rolled his eyes to the ceiling. "I dreamed about these fries while I was eating boiled goat in Somalia."

"Is that all you dreamed about?" All she'd been dreaming about since they made love was a repeat performance, but since she'd taken up residence at the McClintock ranch, they'd only exchanged a few furtive kisses.

He stopped mid-chew, a smudge of ketchup on the corner of his mouth. Julia extended her hand and dabbed the ketchup with the tip of her finger. Then she sucked the ketchup from her fingertip and she didn't even like ketchup.

Ryder swallowed his food and then took a long draw from his iced tea. "The Miner's french fries and sex."

Her brows shot up. "In that order?"

"At the same time."

Ryder's low chuckle ignited a flame in her belly and she choked out, "At the same…"

She jumped as the chair next to her scraped against the wood floor and Rafe straddled it. He hung over the back and snatched a fry from Ryder's plate.

"Ugh, why do you have to ruin them by soaking them in ketchup?" He dropped the fry back on Ryder's plate and dusted his hands together.

"Have you located Charlie yet?" Ryder scooted the fry Rafe touched off his plate.

"Nope, and Gracie is kicking up a fuss. She insists her baby boy is lying injured and near death somewhere, a victim of the killer who strangled Rosie."

Julia gulped and twisted a napkin on the table. She'd had the same feeling. "Do you have any evidence linking Charlie to Rosie's murder?"

"Other than the fact that he had the hots for her and she was probably just leading him on?" Rafe shrugged. "No. Whoever did this covered his tracks. No clear footprints, no evidence left on the body that we can detect, no witnesses."

"But you have Brody's card."

"Which we think she was about to give to my big brother here. But without the info as to where she got that card, it's useless." He cocked an eyebrow at Ryder. "You're sure she didn't give you any names over the phone?"

"You think I wouldn't tell you?" Ryder finished the last of his burger, wiped his mouth with a napkin and tossed it onto his ketchup-smeared plate. "No name. She wanted the cash first, but you're not going to pass that tidbit along to Ballard, are you?"

Rafe shook his head and then bestowed his boyish grin on the waitress. "Could you please bring me an order of fries and a glass of lemonade?"

Folding his arms across the back of the chair, Rafe said, "Sheriff Ballard has checked out. He turned most of this investigation over to me and Duke Lambert, and I'm sure we'll have the rest of the San Juan County Sheriff's Department descending on us soon. They've already taken over Zack's murder."

"Yeah, I know. They questioned me about the attack the night of Zack's murder." Julia rubbed the goose bumps that popped up on her arms. Every time she thought about that night, a tide of dark fear swept through her body. The ether-soaked cloth made it clear her assailant had something other than murder in store for her.

"Are you all right?" Ryder clasped her shoulder with warm, strong fingers, banishing the terror that engulfed her.

She felt safe in his presence, in his family's home. But what if the Sheriff's Department couldn't catch this maniac before Ryder left for parts unknown? She and Shelby couldn't stay with his family, not without the cocoon of security Ryder offered. She couldn't face this threat alone, didn't want to.

"I'm fine." She shoved back from the table. "I have to get back to the shop to help Maddie. We were in the middle of inventory."

"After I help Rod with some projects around the ranch, I'm going out to your house to check the tapes from the cameras. Do you need anything?"

"I'll meet you there when we close up the shop at six o'clock. Shelby's been asking for a few toys she left behind."

Julia left the two brothers at the table and stood on the sidewalk, blinking in the bright sunlight. Summer tourists back from morning hikes or fishing or the train ride to Durango thronged Silverhill's main street, ducking in and out of restaurants and souvenir shops. They laughed and licked ice-cream cones and sipped wine, unaware of Rosie's murder, and only slightly uneasy about the murder of a sheriff's deputy.

Once the news about the murder got out, the Silverhill Chamber of Commerce would whir into action. Silverhill prided itself on its quaint, hometown reputation far from the glittery crowds at Aspen. Two murders in the space of a week just torpedoed hometown quaintness.

And the city fathers could thank her for that.

RYDER POPPED the disc out of the camera and slid a new one into the slot. Then he rearranged the dried leaves of the plant to hide the camera. A few of the leaves broke apart in his hand and he brushed off the debris against the seat of his jeans. Julia had really taken his advice to heart when he told her not to water the plants.

Her car pulled up to the house and she jumped out, tugging at her short, flirty skirt. The light sweater that topped her skirt hugged her body and revealed a sliver of skin on her flat stomach. Her dark hair danced loosely about her shoulders.

Since recovering her memories, Julia had been dressing more stylishly, more like the old Julia. But a fundamental difference remained. This Julia had a daughter. His daughter. Motherhood had softened her sharp edges.

She waved, her eyes widening. "Everything okay? Have you looked at the tapes yet?"

He snapped his mouth shut. He'd been gawking. "I just switched them. Haven't had a chance to view them yet."

Not that the cameras had been any use. After they installed them, the direct attacks on Julia's home had stopped. No more flowers. No more break-ins. No more dead animals.

Just dead people.

She skipped up the steps, swinging a tote bag from her hand. She held it up. "For Shelby's toys."

He followed her into the house on a cloud of her floral perfume or maybe it wasn't perfume at all. She always smelled like fresh flowers.

As she disappeared into Shelby's room, he swept the disc reader from the top of the TV. "Mind if I watch in here? I'd rather do it here than at the ranch."

She poked her head around the corner, quirking her eyebrows. "Me, too."

He laughed. "Don't give me any ideas, woman."

Her muffled response came from the bedroom as he crouched to slip the disc reader into the DVD player. Perching on the edge of her coffee table, Ryder hunched forward and watched Julia's front porch…which was as exciting as watching a rock erode.

She strolled to his side, clutching two transformer-type figures in her hands. He jerked his thumb at the toys. "Doesn't our daughter play with dolls?"

"Not often. Her new must-haves are horses, thank you very much."

"She's doing great with her riding lessons. She has so much confidence."

"Not too much, I hope. I don't want her taking any foolish chances."

"Not with me watching her." He pointed to the TV screen showing a woman on the porch crouched at the front window. "Who's that?"

They both leaned in closer and Julia snorted. "That's Gracie Malone peering through my window. What did she hope to see since I've been at your parents' ranch?"

He pushed a button on the remote control to freeze the frame and check the time stamp. Yesterday at five o'clock. Had Charlie gone missing already? He pointed to the window that attracted Gracie. "You need to replace that hardware."

Julia walked to the front window where she had laid her curtain rod across a loose bracket. She reached up, trying to wedge the curtain rod tighter against the broken bracket and jumped back as the entire bracket fell out of the wall and the rod almost hit her on the head.

"Not much for home repairs, are you? You just made it worse. Now the whole window on the right is uncovered."

"It's not like I've been around to get anything fixed." She rested the curtain rod on the floor. "I'll tack a sheet up before I leave."

She dropped onto the couch to his left and propped her feet up on the coffee table, tapping his hip with her toe. "What's she doing now?"

"Nothing. She peeked in the window and then turned around and left." He fast-forwarded through the frames of empty activity. "Maybe she was looking for Charlie."

"The buzz has hit the town. The news of Rosie's death and Charlie's disappearance spread faster than an avalanche. Some of the tourists are convinced there's a crazed killer on the loose."

"There is, but…" Ryder stopped and clenched his jaw.

Julia's foot froze and her brown eyes grew big and glassy. She knotted her hands in front of her and seemed to shrink two sizes. She finished his sentence. "But the crazed killer isn't after tourists. He's after me and those who dare to get in the way of his objective."

"I'm sorry." Ryder launched off the coffee table and landed next to her on the couch. He grabbed her hands and tried to knead out the cold. "That was a dumb thing to say."

"Insensitive maybe, but not dumb. Unfortunately, it's the truth."

He ran his hands up her arms and squeezed her shoulders. "Maybe you should just get away from here for a while. You don't have any classes until September, and Millie can get someone to fill in for you at the shop."

"I am getting away."

Even though he'd just suggested it himself, Julia's words hit him like a cold splash of water. "You're leaving Silverhill?"

"My mother called me this afternoon after I saw you. You know how emotional she is, but this time guilt and sadness fueled her emotions, not anger. She felt horrible that I was here in Colorado with no memory for four years with her granddaughter and she did nothing to find me or try to reach me." Julia pleated the hem of her skirt with trembling fingers. "I think she was sincere."

"So you're going to Paris?" The steadiness of his voice amazed him because shards of emotions ripped through his body.

She nodded, her gaze pinned to her busy fingers.

"When?"

"Next week."

"You're leaving for Paris in a week and taking Shelby with you?" Because he was still clenching his teeth, the words came out angrier than he intended.

Julia jerked up her head, her fierce stare singeing his skin. "And is that before or after you're leaving, Ryder? Don't think for a minute I've missed those furtive phone calls you've been having. It was the same in Paris, but I didn't see the signs then. I didn't want to see them. It's very clear now."

Clear? How could it be clear to her when he couldn't even sift through the muck in his brain? He didn't want her to leave him. "How can you go to Paris? You need passports."

His words rang with petty satisfaction. He couldn't help it. He had to grasp at any detail to keep her here.

Her brows snapped together, her hands fisting in the folds of her skirt. "Who are you, my travel agent? We have everything we need to leave the country."

"I don't want you to leave." He gripped her shoulders, his

fingers pinching into her skin through the soft material of her sweater.

Julia twisted out of his grasp, her chin tilting in a challenge. "You just told me to get out of Silverhill."

"Not to go to Paris…alone." He raked his fingers through his tangled hair. "I bought a little place in South Carolina, on the coast. I planned to settle you and Shelby there until this all blows over, until…"

"Until what? Until you come back from Zimbabwe or Venezuela or Timbuktu? Maybe if you're lucky, I'll lose my memory again. That'll give you more time to figure out if you want to make a commitment to a family or not." Her bottom lip quivered and her eyes bright with anger a moment ago, now glistened with tears.

Damn, he'd made a mess of things. When he discovered Julia living here, he'd set out to make her love him again, selfishly. He never considered the fallout when it was time to take up his next assignment.

Wrapping his arms around her, Ryder drew her into a tight embrace. She bucked and arched like an unbroken filly until he took possession of her lips, salty from the tears rolling down her face.

As he deepened his kiss, her fingers clawed at his hair, digging into his scalp. She drew his bottom lip between her teeth and nipped at it. He welcomed the pain, welcomed her punishment as she pummeled him with her ferocious love.

Julia straddled Ryder and pushed him against the cushions of the couch, hating him, hating herself for wanting him with a potent need that overruled every ounce of common sense she possessed.

He responded like she knew he would. His hands curled around her hips, and he ground her against the erection that strained against his tight jeans.

She yanked up his T-shirt and pulled it over his head as he raised his arms. Her fingernails skimmed across his smooth, bare chest, trailing over the hard ridge of muscle that tensed beneath her touch.

His hands scrambled beneath her skirt and grabbed her panties. With one strong tug, he ripped them from her body. Gasping, she fell against his chest and burrowed into his shoulder, her lips pressed against the pulse that thrummed in his throat. She inhaled the scent of maleness that rose from his body in heady waves, fueling her passion.

His fingers circled her swollen flesh once before sliding into her wet core. A flash of heat claimed her body at the strong desire she felt for him even as she fought with him. But the shame lasted for only seconds as she cupped her hand around the bulge in his jeans.

Leaning back, she tore at the buttons of his fly. She shifted to the side as he lifted his hips and peeled off his jeans where they bunched around his muscular thighs. He hadn't even bothered with underwear. His hard desire, smooth and pulsing, sprang forward in full readiness.

They couldn't wait to undress. They couldn't wait for words. If Ryder had to leave her, then damn it, she'd give him a final taste of what he'd be missing while he gnawed on boiled goat.

Shoving her ripped panties to the side, she lowered herself on him, but he couldn't wait. He thrust up, spearing her, filling her up with his primal need to completely possess her. They rode each other, their bodies at the point of their ultimate connection, slick with sweat.

He ran the pad of his thumb across her thick, honeyed flesh as he continued to pound into her. Her sweet climax claimed her, gripping her in its talons of pleasure over and over. As she cried out her final release, Ryder roared, arching his back, filling her womb with his seed.

She rested her head against his thundering heart as her hot, ragged breath moistened his skin. Sighing, she opened her eyes, her unfocused gaze settling on the window with the curtains askew. She screamed and rolled off Ryder's body, yanking her skirt down.

Charlie Malone's face, pale and wide-eyed, had floated at the window for just a second.

Chapter Fourteen

Ryder, reclining against the couch half-naked, jerked forward, his knees bumping the coffee table. "What's wrong?"

Julia covered her mouth with one hand to stifle a second scream and pointed a shaking finger toward the window. "Charlie."

Grabbing his jeans, Ryder scrambled from the couch, almost toppling over as his pants wrapped around his legs. He swore and Julia let loose with a high-pitched, hysterical giggle. He scowled at her and yanked up his pants.

"Charlie was at the window?"

"Yeah, I saw his face a-after, when w-we…"

"I get it." He charged toward the front door, buttoning his fly and Julia hung on to his arm.

"Where are you going?"

His brows shot up. "I'm going after Charlie."

"Don't go." She squeezed his bicep, digging her nails into him with panic, not passion, this time. "Don't leave me, Ryder."

Sparks flared in his blue eyes. He crushed her against his bare chest, still damp with the sweat from their shared lovemaking. He murmured into her tangled hair, "I'll never leave you again.

"But I need to go after Charlie." Peeling her hands from his body, Ryder kissed the top of her head. "Lock the door behind me and don't open it until I return, and call 911."

As soon as Ryder barreled through the front gate, Julia slammed the door shut and locked it. She grabbed her phone and called 911, telling them the man the Sheriff's Department sought for questioning in Rosie Fletcher's death just peered into her window.

She leaned against the window where Charlie's face had appeared, rubbing her arms as she stared into the purple dusk that crawled over the mountains. Fear nibbled at her insides as she imagined all sorts of horrible endings to this drama. What if Charlie had a gun or a knife? Ryder had sailed out of here without a weapon. Hell, he hardly had any clothes on.

Headlights swept the street as a car rolled to a stop in front of her house. Her stomach clenched and she leaned her forehead against the smooth glass of the window to peer at the car.

She let out a long, ragged breath. The San Juan County Sheriff's Department. Duke Lambert swung through the gate and ambled up the walkway, his sunglasses shoved to the top of his head.

Julia's mouth went dry. Why was Duke wearing sunglasses at sunset? She shook her head as Duke's knock resounded through the house. *You're being paranoid.*

She unlocked the door, edging around Duke's bulky frame to look for Ryder. Still not back.

"Hey, Julia. So you saw Charlie Malone at your window?"

"Yeah, at that one to the left." She jerked her thumb in the direction of the window.

Duke tramped through her grass and her flower bed with his cowboy boots to inspect the window. He returned to the porch and lifted a shoulder. "From the flattened flowers it looks like someone was there."

Julia rolled her eyes. "You mean the flowers were trampled before you trampled them?"

"Yeah." His eyes widened at her tone.

Nobody in Silverhill expected Julia Stoker to fight back, but she was Julia Rousseau now and she didn't take crap from anyone.

"I'll dust the window ledge for prints."

"You don't need to do that. I told you it was Charlie at that window."

"Are you going to let me in?" Duke gestured toward the entrance she'd been blocking with her body. She glanced toward the street once more before swinging the door open.

Duke stepped across the threshold and glanced around the room. "The 911 call said someone went after Charlie."

"Ryder. He's still out there looking for him."

"Did Ryder see Charlie at the window, too?" Duke's gaze tracked across the living room and stumbled on her ripped panties hanging off the edge of the coffee table.

A wave of heat surged from her chest to her cheeks. "N-no."

"Too busy, huh?" His eyes shifted to Ryder's T-shirt crumpled into a ball and stuck in the cushion of the couch, before lingering on her panties. "Maybe it wasn't Charlie at all. Maybe it was just a garden-variety Peeping Tom enjoying the show."

"You pig."

Duke smirked. "No wonder you have stalkers after you."

The titillation lighting his eyes turned her stomach and she clenched her hands into fists.

The half-open front door crashed against the wall, and they both jumped. In two long strides, Ryder ate up the distance between him and Duke and grabbed him by the throat.

Duke's eyes popped out of their sockets as Ryder drew his fist back, the corded muscles of his arm visible and lethal. Duke choked out, "You can't assault a sheriff's deputy."

"Get the hell out of here." Ryder shoved him, and Duke

stumbled backward. "I'm filing a complaint with your department."

Duke's chubby cheeks reddened. "I didn't mean anything, Ryder."

"Get out."

When he reached the door, Duke threw a glance over his shoulder. "Did you find Charlie?"

Ryder crossed his arms over his chest, his legs in a wide stance, his lips a thin line. His taut, hard muscles signaled danger and Duke scurried out the front door without waiting for an answer.

Ryder swung toward Julia and cupped her face in his rough hands. "Are you all right?"

She snorted. "Did you think I was going to let that horse's ass stand there and say those things to me without letting him have it?"

She'd been ready to lay into Duke herself, but Ryder's protection sure felt good…and it totally turned her on. Not that she needed any more stimuli from Ryder to get her hot. Just feasting her eyes on the man's bare torso with the planes of muscle across his chest and the tight six-pack abs was enough to send her into a swoon. It didn't help that he'd never gotten around to fastening the top button of his jeans, which hung precariously low on his hips.

"I knew you wouldn't accept that treatment from Duke or anyone else." He kissed her lips. "I was just trying to protect Duke from your wrath."

Skimming her hands down his back, she kissed him and then shot a sideways glance at the window, still uncovered. "I take it you didn't find Charlie?"

"No, I didn't. I wonder if his mother's hiding him somewhere."

"I don't think Gracie would hide a killer, especially someone who killed Zack Ballard, even Charlie."

"Maybe the stalking and the murders are unrelated." He hooked an arm around her shoulders. "Maybe Charlie really did murder Zack in a jealous rage over Rosie and then murdered Rosie because he thought she was meeting me as a lover."

"And the phone call to me from Zack's phone and Dr. Brody's card in Rosie's possession were just coincidences? I think they're all linked."

He shrugged. "I think you and Shelby need to get out of town, whether that's Paris or…somewhere else. Now let's get this place closed up and head back to the ranch."

His hand slid to her bottom and his warmth connected with her skin through the thin material of her skirt, curling her toes and weakening her knees. God help her, she wanted him again.

Even with the fear and uncertainty folding around her like a heavy cape, she wanted him again.

HE DIDN'T DESERVE a family. He specialized in breaking up families. If he'd kept his mouth shut about seeing his father with Pam all those years ago, his mother would've stayed. She knew about her husband's philandering, but confronted with it in front of her family, she had to save face and walk out. But she didn't just walk out on her husband, she walked out on her family. Ryder did that.

And what about Julia's marriage to Jeremy?

He'd torpedoed that, too. When he first met her and felt that strong attraction rock him to his core, he should've bowed out. He should've left Paris. Instead he hung around and stoked the embers of their passion. Maybe Julia and Jeremy could've stayed together and worked through their problems. Maybe Jeremy never would've turned traitor.

Julia's desire for Ryder put her in harm's way. She'd gone to Tucson to protect him. He didn't deserve a family.

Ryder buried his fingers in his hair. If he walked out now, took that next assignment, he could escape the weight of responsibility of keeping a family together. He could take the easy way out.

He grabbed the phone and tapped it against his forehead.

"Is that a new way to make a call?" Rafe ambled into the room, peeling an orange.

The spray from the orange peel arced up and sprinkled the edge of Rod's spotless desk.

Dropping the phone, Ryder tilted his chin at the film of moisture on the shiny wood. "He's gonna kill you."

"He'll never know." Rafe ran his palm across the orange juice, smearing it into a sticky circle.

"Yeah, right. Any news on Charlie?"

"Still missing. You didn't mention a car two nights ago at Julia's. If he got away on foot, he can't be far."

"Anyone check the caves at The Twirling Ballerinas?"

"I took a quick look, but we don't have the manpower for that. There's no clear evidence linking Charlie to Rosie's murder or Zack's. We just want him for questioning."

"If I can keep Julia under lock and key for another week and a half, she'll be home free."

"Why a week and a half?" Rafe popped an orange wedge in his mouth.

"She and Shelby are going to Paris."

Rafe swallowed and wiped the back of his hand across his mouth. "She is?"

"Her mother invited her. I think it's good for her to get away. Maybe this maniac, whether it's Charlie or not, will fixate on someone else and you guys can catch him before Julia returns. If Julia returns."

"You're letting Julia get away? What about Shelby?"

"You're leaving your family?" Rod's low voice from the

door startled both of his brothers. Ryder slid his feet from Rod's desk and Rafe hid the orange behind his back.

"I have another assignment." Ryder stiffened his back.

"That's BS. What happened to that private security firm you and your friend wanted to start in Denver? Now would be a perfect time."

"Maybe after this assignment." Ryder avoided Rod's piercing stare.

"So you are leaving your family. Just like Mom."

Ryder jumped up and the chair flew back, hitting the large window that looked out on the McClintock ranch. "Mom had to leave. She had to leave once I told her about Dad's involvement with Pam. Don't blame Mom. Blame me. I ripped this family apart by opening my big mouth."

"There's plenty of blame to go around." Rod's eyes narrowed. "But you don't own any of it. Dad had been fooling around for years before Pam, and Mom knew it. Your acute ten-year-old observation that Dad was kissing the new ski instructor gave Mom the excuse she needed."

"You're the one who spilled the beans?" Rafe's mouth dropped open.

"Shut up, Rafe." Rod dismissed him with a flick of the hand. "Stop protecting Mom, Ryder. She left because she wanted to leave. She never liked the ranch and having three boys in the space of six years was too much for her to handle. She was a lousy mom even before she left without a backward glance."

The truth of Rod's words sliced through him like a knife and then twisted in his gut. He clenched his hands into white-knuckled fists. All these years it had been easier to blame himself for his mother's desertion.

If only he hadn't gone skiing that day with his friends. If only he hadn't been at the lodge the precise moment that Dad kissed

Pam. If only he hadn't told his mother and the rest of the family what he saw.

The truth yawned before him like an endless pit of fear, so deep it threatened to swallow him whole. His mother didn't love her sons. She'd been incapable of love. That's why his father sought solace in the arms of other women.

Ryder ground his teeth together. He'd grown up with two bad examples of parenting. Why would he be any better?

"You blame yourself for Sharon high-tailing it out of here?" Rafe shook his head. "I didn't know that. I could've set you straight. Sharon didn't have a maternal bone in her body."

"Stop." Ryder held up his hands. "I don't need to hear any more from you two. And if you think you made me feel any better about taking on the responsibilities of parenthood, you didn't."

Rod shrugged. "I'm not here to make you feel better, but if you walk out of that little girl's life, you'll be repeating a pattern." He strode toward the door and then twisted his head over his shoulder. "And clean up that crap on my desk, Rafe."

JULIA PEEKED OUT the front window of the antique shop and let out a relieved sigh. Ryder's truck idled at the curb in front of the store.

He'd said all the right words the other night when they made love, but had distanced himself from her and Shelby in the days following. He must've decided to leave them. She heaved another sigh, but relief had nothing to do with it.

"Is your ride here?" Millie's daughter, Maddy, leaned over the counter and winked. "Wish I had a personal escort and bodyguard."

"No, you don't." Julia waved at Ryder and backed away from the window to retrieve her purse behind the counter. "That would mean you have some crazed stalker after you."

"I know." Maddy patted Julia's shoulder. "I'm sorry all this crap is happening to you. Seems like you just can't get a break...until now." She tilted her chin toward the window and Ryder's truck.

Julia swung her bag over her shoulder and said good-bye to Maddy. Did Ryder represent a break or just a broken heart?

As she approached the truck, Ryder jumped out and opened the door. She climbed into the seat and he slammed the door and jogged around to the other side.

"Did you have a good morning? No incidents?" He cranked on the engine and glanced over his left shoulder into oncoming traffic.

"None. No news on Charlie?"

"None."

"Did you and Shelby do anything this morning?"

"I took her to see the horses, but I didn't have time to give her a riding lesson."

She winced, emitting a whimper from the back of her throat. She hadn't imagined it, this distance Ryder was putting between them.

"I had to help Rod with some stuff around the ranch." He kept his gaze pinned to the road ahead. "Are you all set for Paris?"

She swallowed and lifted her chin. "Yeah, we're ready, but I'm afraid my mother is going to faint when she sees my clothes."

Ryder pursed his lips, two deep lines forming at the sides of his mouth. She'd meant to ease the tension between them with a little humor, but he wasn't smiling.

"Celeste is not very motherly." Ryder frowned in concentration as if choosing and then discarding words. He dragged in a breath and blew it out, puffing his cheeks. "Aren't you afraid you'll be the same kind of mother to Shelby? That you'll fail her?"

Her heart jumped, her fingers curling over the edge of the seat.

She didn't like the direction of his questions. Did he just accuse her of being an unfit mother because of the poor example her own mother set? From what she'd heard about Sharon McClintock, he didn't have a lot of wiggle room in this argument.

Beneath lowered lashes, her gaze shifted to the side. Ryder stared straight ahead, his shoulders stiff, his face tight. He looked…scared. She'd never seen Ryder afraid of anything or anyone.

Her pulse ticked against her throat. Could he be frightened of a little, thirty-eight-pound girl?

"You know…" She turned down the radio. "You don't have to have a model parent to be a model parent. Sometimes you just feel it here." She pounded her chest with her fist.

"I may not always make the right choices as a parent, but whatever I do comes from a deep, never-ending pool of love. And somehow Shelby knows that." She trailed her fingers along the corded muscle of his forearm, and he loosened his grip on the steering wheel.

"Trust yourself, Ryder."

The truck swung through the gates of the McClintock ranch, and as they rounded the last bend toward the house, Julia squinted out the window at a clutch of people gathered in the riding paddock. She pointed. "What's going on?"

"I don't know. Let's find out." Ryder pulled the truck over and jumped to the ground.

Several faces turned in their direction, and Pam peeled away from the group and ran toward them.

Julia's heart skittered in her chest at Pam's face, creased with worry. Her gaze darted across the empty paddock, and she clutched Ryder's arm.

"What's wrong, Pam?" Ryder covered Julia's hand with his own.

"It's Shelby. That silly, headstrong little girl rode her pony out of the paddock when Jock wasn't looking." Pam's white fingers plucking at the edge of her blouse gave lie to her light-hearted words.

Julia blinked her eyes, her mouth so dry she couldn't form any words.

"What the hell are you talking about?" Ryder charged to the paddock, and Julia clung to his arm, her rubbery legs unable to support her.

A few of the ranch hands and Ryder's father lifted worried faces at their approach.

"What happened?" The ranch hands shrank back in the face of Ryder's fury.

"Don't worry, boy." Ralph slapped Ryder on the back. "The little gal just got adventurous and took her pony for a real ride."

Ryder shrugged him off. "Will someone tell me what happened here?"

Pam stepped forward. "Shelby wanted a riding lesson and because you weren't around, Jock took her out. He had her seated on Silverbell, and she was circling the paddock. Dan called him over for a minute and when he turned around, she was gone."

Julia broke away from Ryder as fear fueled her senses. She ran toward the open gate of the paddock that led to several horse trails. "Shelby!"

Ralph called after her, "Rod and Jock went after her. She couldn't have gone too far."

"They'll find her." Ryder came up behind her and rested his hands on her shoulders. He slid his hands down her arms and took her hand, leading her back to the group in the middle of the paddock. "Of all the dumb, irresponsible things to do. She's not even supposed to be riding Silverbell. Skipper's her mount."

Julia leaned against Ryder's strong shoulder, closing her

eyes against the panic that overwhelmed her. Why would Shelby ride out of the paddock by herself? How did she get the gate open? She didn't want to acknowledge the black terror that scratched at the edges of her mind.

"She's going to be all right." Ryder cupped her face in his hands, and she raised her eyes to meet his.

She recoiled at the depths of fear lurking in his eyes. They mirrored the same dark dread that clutched at her heart.

Pam gasped and Julia tore her gaze away from Ryder's. Rod and Jock burst into the paddock, leading a skittish Silverbell behind them.

And her saddle was empty.

Chapter Fifteen

Julia swayed and she threw out her hands to regain her balance. Ryder started to charge his brother and then spun around to catch Julia before she collapsed in the dirt. He hooked an arm around her waist, pressing his side against hers as if the two of them could defeat this threat to their daughter together.

"Where's Shelby?" His voice grated against the shocked silence.

"We don't know." Rod pocketed his cell phone. "We found Silverbell wandering back to the paddock on one of the trails. We followed the trail back into the hills, but didn't find Shelby."

"C-could she have fallen off the trail? Down a cliff?" Julia pressed the heels of her hands against her temples.

"I don't see how she could've gotten to that point on the trail where it drops off. Jock said he took his eyes off of her for just a minute and then went right after her." Rod rubbed a hand across his jaw, his eyes puzzled. "But I called the Sheriff's Department and they're sending over a search and rescue unit."

"Why did you take her out?" Ryder's fists bunched at his sides. "I'm the only one who gives her riding lessons."

Jock lifted a shoulder. "I'm sorry, Ryder. You were busy this morning, and Pam said it was okay."

Ryder crossed his arms, shoving his fists into his biceps. "I have to find her."

"I'm going with you." Julia followed him across the dusty paddock to the yawning gate, and he latched it behind them. She ran to keep up with Ryder's long stride. "Wait."

He turned and she flinched at the despair in his eyes.

She gave voice to the fear that had been nipping at her mind like a rabid dog. "Don't you think it's strange that Shelby opened that gate and rode away from Jock, disappearing from Silverbell's back in a matter of minutes?"

A muscle twitched in his jaw. "That's not how it happened and you know it. Someone took her."

Julia cried out as the blunt truth slammed against her chest. Ryder gripped her hands.

"I'm sorry. It's my fault." His shoulders slumped as he dropped his gaze to the ground.

She'd never seen Ryder defeated and it made her mad as hell. She needed him now like she never had before. She squeezed his hands. "Stop. It's not your fault. As a parent, you can't be with your child twenty-four hours a day. You can't cave in to a child's every whim. If we're playing the blame game here, then most of it's right on my shoulders. I attracted this stalker somehow. I let him into our lives."

Ryder straightened his shoulders and gave her a little shake. "Let's put the blame where it belongs—on this maniac who's been terrorizing you and has now snatched Shelby. And let's deal with him."

"How? We don't know where he is. We don't even know who he is. It could be Charlie. It could be one of those nut jobs who came out of the woodwork when my story broke. It could be a stranger. How are we going to find him and deal with him?"

"He'll find you, Julia. We both know what he wants and it's

not Shelby. She's just a means to an end, just like Brody, just like Zack, just like Rosie."

"He wants me."

A chill zinged up her spine and she hunched her shoulders. Ryder pulled her into his arms, which represented her only safe harbor these days. He weaved his fingers through her hair, pulling her head back to look into her face.

"We'll get her back and then I'll keep both of you safe forever…or die trying."

By the set of his jaw and the fire in his eyes, Julia knew he meant every word. "How do you think he'll contact me?"

"How has he always contacted you?"

"My house."

RYDER LET the search and rescue team carry on, but he knew they wouldn't find Shelby at the bottom of a ravine. He drove Julia to her house with the excuse to the others that he and Julia had a few places to search.

When they swung through her front gate, disappointment stabbed his gut when he saw the empty porch. He figured the man who kidnapped Shelby might have left Julia another message on her porch.

"Nothing's here." Julia stumbled on the first step and Ryder grabbed her around the waist. Then she pulled her shoulders back and planted her feet on the ground. "Should we leave and give him another chance or do you think he expects an ambush now?"

He admired her courage in the face of this crippling blow. After that first moment of anguish, she'd been handling Shelby's abduction better than he'd been coping.

"Maybe we should ambush him."

"No! He still has Shelby."

Julia's cell phone rang and as she reached for it, Ryder

gripped her arm and said, "Don't tell the Sheriff's Department anything yet. We don't want to spook the guy by having the police trampling along the trails looking for him."

Before she answered the phone, she glanced at the incoming number. Gasping, she held the phone out for him to see.

The display read, *Zack*.

Ryder hissed, "It's him. He still has Zack's cell phone."

"Hello?" Julia covered her mouth, her eyes wide above her hand. "Yes. Yes. I won't." She paused. "Don't hurt her."

She snapped the phone shut and hugged herself. That was his job. He wrapped his arms around her stiff body. "What did he say? Was it Charlie?"

"I—I don't think so. His voice was low, almost a whisper. I didn't recognize it, but then I don't think he wanted me to."

"Is Shelby okay?" He held his breath. If anything happened to his daughter, he'd rip this guy apart with his bare hands.

"She sounds fine. I heard her in the background."

"What does he want you to do?"

"He wants me to meet him at The Twirling Ballerinas." A tremble rolled through her frame. "Alone."

"Like hell."

"Once he has me, he'll send Shelby back."

"Police?"

"No. He said he knows what the San Juan County Sheriff's Department is doing at all times. If he suspects any police involvement he'll…" She buried her face in his chest.

"Did he mention me?"

Pulling away from him, she tilted her head, the setting sun catching a single tear sparkling on her dark lashes. "No. Isn't that odd? Whether or not it's Charlie, he must know about your involvement. He slashed your tires."

"When are you supposed to meet him?"

"Right now. I have to leave now."

"*We* have to leave now." He had no intention of allowing Julia to walk into this alone and trade herself for Shelby. He planned to save his daughter, protect Julia and ground this SOB into the dirt.

"How are you going to stay out of sight? If he knows what the Sheriff's Department is doing, maybe he's watching all of us."

"He probably has a police scanner." He smoothed her hair back from her face. "And don't forget, these trails and mountains served as my playground when I was growing up. Nobody knows them like the McClintocks."

"Charlie?"

"Moved here as a teenager when his father died. He's not a local."

Julia smoothed her palms across his chest, the anxious lines on her face retreating. "I trust you, Ryder."

He pressed his lips against her smooth cheek. She had a helluva lot more faith in him than he did in himself, but the full measure of her trust made him believe he could slay dragons for his family.

Ten minutes later, Ryder clambered up the side of a cliff, taking the shortcut and a rough path one level above and parallel to The Twirling Ballerinas Trail. He'd traded his boots for a pair of running shoes he had stashed in his truck and crept silently along the pathway, tangled with underbrush and rock.

He followed Julia, occasionally catching sight of her red sweatshirt in the gathering darkness on the trail below him. Once she reached the clearing with the three towering pinnacles of rock known as The Twirling Ballerinas, he crouched in a hollowed-out boulder, which gave him a clear view of the expanse of ground below.

Julia stepped into the clearing, facing the fantastic rock formations, and cried out, "Hello? It's Julia. I'm here. Where's my daughter?"

"Over here." A man's voice, deepened by the acoustics of the caves called back.

Ryder's gut clenched. The man was in the labyrinth of caves behind The Twirling Ballerinas. Had he been hiding out here all along? Ryder and his brothers knew this spot well, but not even they could always navigate their way through the twists and turns of the endless caverns.

Julia glanced over her shoulder once before disappearing into the dark mouth of the cave entrance. Ryder scrambled from his hiding place and searched for the hole that would drop him into the center of the maze of caves below him.

This guy couldn't be a local if he didn't know this other, secret entrance to the caves.

Chewing his lower lip, he eyed the gap in the rocks that led to the caves. The last time he'd shimmied through that space, he'd been a skinny teenager on his way to warn Rafe that Rod planned to kick his behind for not rubbing down and grooming Rod's horse after riding it.

Sitting on the ground, Ryder poked his feet through the gap and then rolled onto his stomach to squeeze through, using his hands to propel him downward. He pulled his gun out of his waistband and clutched it in one hand and then sucked in his breath to push himself farther down. His legs dangled below him and the hole swallowed him up to his armpits.

He was stuck, the rocks painfully gouging him under his arms. His scratched hands found leverage and he shoved against a ridge in the earth as he pumped his legs. With one final push, his shoulders popped through the opening as his face raked against the rock. A sharp edge of stone caught his hand, jarring the gun loose. Ryder made a last grab for his weapon before losing it.

Now he knew what a newborn felt coming through the birth canal.

He hit the ground with a thud and leaned against the damp walls of the cave, inhaling the smell of dank earth as his heart slammed in his chest.

He waited while his eyes adjusted to the gloom. He couldn't exactly whip out a flashlight and a ledge of rock obscured the light from the hole above. His nostrils flared. He smelled spicy cologne and he knew Julia didn't wear that fragrance.

They must be close.

With his hand trailing along the cave wall, Ryder hunched forward and moved toward a murmur of sound. Voices. He closed his eyes for a moment, dizzy from the relief.

He brushed his fingers against three stalactites extending from the ceiling of the cave and knew exactly where he stood. A large clearing opened up just around the next bend. They'd called it Rafe's Retreat because Rafe used to bring his girl-friends here to make out.

Licking his lips, Ryder eased forward and crouched on the ground, wedging his body between two wet rocks to peer through a crack. Even if he'd still had his weapon, the opening was too small for the barrel of a gun and too small to see anything.

Tilting his head back, he gazed at the rocks leading up to the top of the cave. There was an overhang rimming the little room, and if he could make it up there, it would afford him a good view.

Ryder climbed the rocks, his hands and feet slipping on the moss. He scrambled to the top, hauling himself over the last edge and lay panting for a few moments. The hum of voices below reminded him of the urgency of his mission.

On his hands and knees, he crawled to the edge of the opening and hunched behind a rock, peering into the clearing.

A kerosene lamp lit the little room, casting a circle of eerie, waxy light on the three frozen figures in its center. Shelby lay on a pallet by the wall and Julia was kneeling beside her. A man with his back to Ryder extended a gun in front of him, pointing it at Shelby.

Heated blood fueled by rage pounded against Ryder's ears. He wanted to take out the SOB here and now, and if it turned out to be Charlie, he'd crush him before turning him over to the Sheriff's Department. Ryder cocked his head. Couldn't be Charlie—too skinny.

"Is she all right?" Julia ran her hand across Shelby's brow.

The man answered, "She was tired after that riding lesson and the hike up here. She fell asleep on her own."

The man's voice chilled Ryder's blood. It couldn't be and yet there was something so familiar about his stance. Ryder lay flat on his stomach and shimmied to the opening.

He held his breath as the man turned to the side, adjusting his sunglasses. When the man lowered his hand, the light fell across his face. Nausea twisted Ryder's gut.

Somehow he escaped.

Somehow he was alive.

And now Jeremy Scott had Ryder's daughter at gunpoint.

JULIA SMOOTHED Shelby's curls from her pink cheek. When the stranger with the sunglasses emerged from the cave, her fear doubled and it had nothing to do with the gun he was brandishing. If he had been Charlie or someone she knew, she could reason with him. But she didn't stand a chance with this stranger in sunglasses.

She had faith in Ryder. She just hoped he could find that faith in himself.

Curling her fingers around Shelby's, she turned toward the stranger. "Why me? Did you read about me in the newspapers? Did you see me in Dr. Brody's office?"

The man smiled and if he weren't pointing a gun at Shelby, she'd find the smile almost charming. He shook his head. "I thought you'd regained your memory with the help of the gallant Ryder."

Her breath quickened. Someone from her past. "I have for the most part, but there are still incidents, people, faces I can't recall. Obviously yours is one of them…if you're telling me the truth."

He clicked his tongue. "I'm hurt, but the fact that you don't remember me worked in my favor that night I tried to get you to pull over."

"When the police told me Dr. Brody left the bar in Durango with a man in sunglasses, I made the connection. If I had pulled over that night…" She shivered and clutched Shelby's hand.

"All of those other tricks wouldn't have been necessary." He shrugged in a very French way. "But I enjoyed it. I like playing games."

"Killing people? You like killing people? You did kill Dr. Brody, Zack and Rosie Fletcher, didn't you? And what about Charlie?"

"Dr. Brody knew too much. And the fact that he wanted you made it easy to set him up and throw you off my trail. The idiot sheriff's deputy discovered I was hiding out here, and Rosie found Brody's card when she rifled my pockets after we slept together. Charlie?" He shrugged. "That moron may have discovered Rosie's body. He used to follow her everywhere, but I have no idea where he is."

Julia swallowed hard. The man was ruthless. Would Ryder

be able to find them in this maze of caves? She had to distract him somehow, get him to take the gun off Shelby to give Ryder a chance to come at him. She hoped Ryder wouldn't come in with his gun blazing. The stranger just might get a shot off first.

"Who are you? What do you want from me?"

"I want you, Julia. You belong to me. I'll take you away from here, and then we'll call Ryder and tell him to pick up his brat."

She gasped. How did he know so much about them?

The man laughed. "Of course, knowing Ryder, he's probably already here somewhere, but if he tries something, his daughter dies."

"Y-you know Ryder, too?"

"Of course I know him. I worked with him."

Julia drew her brows together. "At the agency? With Black Cobra?"

"So you remember that. Ryder would've never told you about Black Cobra. He's such a loyal spy. Not so loyal to his friends, though." The man unbuttoned the cuff of his long-sleeve shirt with his teeth and pulled the sleeve up to his elbow. He thrust his arm in front of him. "Here's the proof."

She pushed off the ground to get a better look at his forearm. He shifted forward so that the circle of light from the kerosene lamp illuminated his arm and the tattoo of the black snake.

Clutching her stomach, Julia stumbled backward. "Jeremy!"

ADRENALINE PUMPED through Ryder's body. Julia knew now. She knew she faced her ex-husband and he was the enemy.

She tilted her head up to gaze into Jeremy's dark sunglasses. He shoved the glasses on top of his head, and she shrank back, pressing her hand over her mouth.

Something close to pity stirred in Ryder's gut. Jeremy's face stretched tightly across his cheekbones, his eyes unnaturally wide and unblinking.

"Not as handsome as I used to be, huh, Julia? But then I guess you don't remember what I looked like anyway."

"You died in the bomb blast. I remember. I remember the house blowing up. I remember the flames."

"Yeah, that fire did a number to my face and my upper body, but I crawled away…no thanks to you. You sped off in that car I stole, taking all my money with you."

"How'd you find me? How long have you been watching me?"

"I heard through my sources that Ryder was finally coming home on leave. I landed in Silverhill before he did and learned all about the mysterious woman with amnesia and a three-year-old daughter." He waved the gun at Shelby's sleeping form. "We can play catch-up later. We need to get going."

Ryder tensed his muscles. He'd have to drop on top of Jeremy before he could get a shot off…before he took Julia away. He drew his knees to his chest and then stopped when he heard Jeremy's voice.

"Wake up, kid."

Ryder bunched his hands into fists. He couldn't attack Jeremy if he had Shelby in his arms.

Pointing the gun at Shelby, Jeremy prodded her with his foot.

"What are you doing?" Julia reached out toward Jeremy, grasping his arm.

He shook her off. "She's coming out with us. Do you think I'm going to walk out of these caves into an ambush without my insurance? Ryder will never come at me as long as I have his daughter."

Ryder wiped a trickle of sweat from his brow. For once in his miserable life, Jeremy was right. Ryder couldn't tackle him if he had Shelby at gunpoint.

Tossing back her hair, Julia let out a throaty purr. "Let's leave her for Ryder, Jeremy. I want to come with you. Why didn't you just come forward when you found me?"

Ryder's heart pounded against his ribcage. Was Julia making her move? Could she see him up here?

"Don't play me, Julia. The last time we saw each other, I'd forced you to come to Arizona to save your boyfriend and discovered you were pregnant with his baby. It ended... badly."

"You never gave me a chance to explain. Finding you with that other woman in Paris devastated me, and Ryder took advantage of the situation. He told me you'd been with a lot of women. He persuaded me to leave you." Her voice hitched in her throat. "I never wanted to leave you, Jeremy."

A muscle ticked in Ryder's jaw. Damn that woman was a good actress...or at least she better be acting.

Jeremy snorted. "So you slept with Ryder because you didn't want to leave me?"

"It was revenge sex." She threw out her hands and Jeremy stepped back, away from Shelby. "I wanted to hurt you, to get back at you. But it was too late. You resigned from the agency and left Paris. When you called me about the computer disc, I jumped at the chance to see you again."

"And then left me to fry in a burning house."

"I was terrified. I thought you were dead and I thought whoever killed you would come after me." She moved closer to Jeremy and ran her hand along his back. "C'mon, baby. You know me better than anyone. You know I never wanted kids. Now that Ryder's back and he knows he's Shelby's father, he can take care of her. And I can take care of you."

Jeremy caught Julia's hand and brought it to his lips. "I have to hand it to you. You're good, but you're going to take care of me whether you want to or not. Now wake her up, so we can get out of here."

Julia kneeled beside Shelby, hunching over her body, shielding her from Jeremy's gun.

Ryder seized the opportunity with both hands and hurled himself over the edge. He dropped on top of Jeremy.

Jeremy grunted and squeezed off a shot, the bullet leaving a trail of heat as it zinged past Ryder's thigh. As he planted a knee on Jeremy's chest, Ryder yelled at Julia, "Get Shelby out of here."

Julia gathered Shelby in her arms, her eyes never leaving the two men grappling on the floor of the cave. She didn't want to leave Ryder with this madman, but she had to find a safe place for Shelby first. She'd come back to help Ryder.

As Julia stumbled through the cave, heading toward the light, Shelby stirred and yawned. Another shot rang out and she sobbed and tripped. A voice echoed in the cave behind her, "Julia."

A chill flashed up her spine. The same voice that haunted her dreams. The same voice that spun out from the leaping flames in Arizona.

Gripping Shelby tighter, Julia burst from the cave and fell to the ground, a sharp pain lancing her ankle. Seconds later, Jeremy stumbled out after her, the gun dangling from his fingers.

Panic, like a wildfire, raced through her body, leaving her light-headed. Ryder. Jeremy shot Ryder in the cave. She howled, the sound gathering in her belly and filling the mountain air with its raw anguish.

Jeremy stopped in his tracks, his lips curling into a smile. He raised both arms to her, the snake on his forearm flexing grotesquely.

Ryder charged out of the mouth of the cave, running straight at Jeremy. Ryder tackled him and they skidded across the dirt, rolling to the edge of the cliff. The force of the hit had jarred the gun from Jeremy's hand and it flew to the side of the grappling bodies.

"Stay here. Don't move." Julia tucked a wide-eyed Shelby into a cubby hole at the cave's entrance. Then she retrieved the gun. With trembling hands, she pointed the weapon at Ryder and Jeremy locked in a life-and-death struggle at the edge of the precipice.

"Jeremy, I have your gun."

Both men looked up in mid-punch and then Ryder shoved away from Jeremy, wiping the back of his hand across his bleeding mouth. "Looks like the game is over, Jeremy. You lose."

"You know how much I hate losing, Ryder." Jeremy cracked a smile then rolled off the edge of the cliff.

Epilogue

Julia traced her fingertip along Jeremy's face, safely captured in a photo and neatly tucked behind the clear plastic sheet in the photo album. Handsome, charming, adventurous—just the tonic she'd needed after Dad's death.

Sighing, she snapped the cover shut and strolled to her mother's balcony. She planted her elbows on the wrought-iron railing entwined with purple wisteria and gazed at the busy Paris boulevard below.

When she arrived in Paris, Julia had waited for the warm, comforting blanket of home to engulf her. Mom, sobered by Julia's experience with amnesia, welcomed her back with open arms and an open heart. Mom dived into her role as *grandmère* with the gusto she usually reserved for Paris fashion week.

Despite her mother's effusive efforts, Julia still didn't feel as if she belonged here…because she belonged with Ryder.

During their struggle in the cave, Jeremy had shot Ryder in the shoulder. Julia wanted to cancel her trip to Paris and stay with Ryder, but he'd insisted she go and take Shelby with her. Was he pushing her out of his life again, pushing his daughter away?

Before Julia left for Paris, Rod pulled her aside and explained to her how much Ryder feared following the bad example set by his parents. How he'd tried to saddle himself with all the blame to avoid admitting his mother never cared for motherhood.

Rod had shrugged his broad shoulders. "He's afraid to be a father. He's afraid to be a husband."

She'd tried to talk to Ryder about it, but she didn't want to push him. She didn't want to coerce him into accepting the role of father if he didn't want it.

She sauntered back into the room, picked up a sofa cushion, and then tossed it aside. With hands on her hips, she surveyed the cheerful room feeling anything but.

The front door of her mother's flat creaked open and Shelby peered around the edge, a perky hat perched on her head at a jaunty, if precarious, angle.

Julia smiled. Her mother had taken her tomboy granddaughter shopping. Boy would she be disappointed when she found that frothy bit of confection floating upside down in a fountain or doubling as a collection basket for rocks.

"Are you back already?"

"I have a surprise." Shelby's curls quivered in excitement as her bright blue eyes danced.

Julia held her breath. She hoped the surprise didn't consist of a muddied kiddy haute couture frock. She didn't want her mother to catch on too quickly that Julia had failed miserably at raising a girly girl.

Shelby shoved the door open to reveal a tall, rangy cowboy, sans hat and boots, filling the doorway of her mother's flat. Julia expelled her breath with a sound that ended halfway between a gurgle and a gasp.

"It's Daddy. We found him outside." Shelby placed her hands on the backs of Ryder's thighs and pushed.

"Ladies shouldn't be pushy, Shelby." Julia's mother popped

up behind Shelby and grabbed her hand. "Come, give your maman and papa time together. Then we can all go out as a family later."

Julia swallowed the lump in her throat as Ryder tousled Shelby's hair, his large hand covering the top of her head.

"I have some things to show you and places to take you that I'm sure your *grandmère* doesn't even know about."

Mom arched a perfect eyebrow. "You're not in Colorado now, Ryder. This little girl needs some civilization, some polish."

Ryder's laugh filled Mom's exquisitely furnished apartments, almost causing the delicate table in the foyer to tremble. "Give it your best shot, Celeste, but Shelby's a Colorado cowgirl. Knew it the minute I spied her on Silverhill's main street."

Julia's mother sent a conspiratorial wink Julia's way before bustling a protesting Shelby, hat and all, down the hallway.

Left alone with Ryder, Julia twisted her hands in front of her although she couldn't pinpoint the source of her nervousness. He came after her, didn't he? Or maybe he just came for Shelby. She dug her heels into Mom's shiny hardwood floor.

"You're awfully quiet."

She tilted her chin. "How's your shoulder?"

"Good as new, except for the bandage." He patted a bulky lump beneath his shirt. "How's Paris?"

Lifting her shoulders, she spread her arms. "It's Paris. What's not to like?"

Actually, she could think of lots of things. First, it wasn't Colorado and second it didn't contain Ryder…until now.

Before she could form the next inane question, Ryder devoured the distance between them in two quick strides and possessed her lips in a fiery, impatient kiss that answered all her questions and settled all her doubts.

When she could breathe and think straight, she whispered against his mouth, "You came for me."

"I always intended to come for you…and our daughter." He cupped her face in his hands, running the pad of his thumb along her throbbing lower lip. "When I confronted the fear of losing you and Shelby in that cave, I knew I'd do everything in my power to protect my family. Even if I failed, I'd die trying."

"You're not going to fail." She kissed that distracting thumb. "You've already given us so much. You gave my life back to me."

"And you've given my life back to me. I resigned from Black Cobra. After all, a married man with a family can't go chasing around the world, running from his fears."

Julia rested her cheek against Ryder's chest, his pounding heart, sure and strong, reverberating through her soul. She felt right at home in his arms and she knew exactly who she was.

She was Julia Rousseau, soon to be Julia McClintock.

And she was loved.

* * * * *

Harlequin is 60 years old,
and Harlequin Blaze is celebrating!
After all, a lot can happen in 60 years,
or 60 minutes…or 60 seconds!
Find out what's going down in Blaze's
heart-stopping new mini-series,
FROM 0 TO 60!
Getting from "Hello" to "How was it?"
can happen fast….

Here's a sneak peek of the first book,
A LONG, HARD RIDE
by Alison Kent
Available March 2009

"IS THAT FOR ME?" Trey asked.

Cardin Worth cocked her head to the side and considered how much better the day already seemed. "Good morning to you, too."

When she didn't hold out the second cup of coffee for him to take, he came closer. She sipped from her heavy white mug, hiding her grin and her giddy rush of nerves behind it.

But when he stopped in front of her, she made the mistake of lowering her gaze from his face to the exposed strip of his chest. It was either give him his cup of coffee or bury her nose against him and breathe in. She remembered so clearly how he smelled. How he tasted.

She gave him his coffee.

After taking a quick gulp, he smiled and said, "Good morning, Cardin. I hope the floor wasn't too hard for you."

The hardness of the floor hadn't been the problem. She shook her head. "Are you kidding? I slept like a baby, swaddled in my sleeping bag."

"In my sleeping bag, you mean."

If he wanted to get technical, yeah. "Thanks for the loaner. It made sleeping on the floor almost bearable." As had the warmth of his spooned body, she thought, then quickly changed the subject. "I saw you have a loaf of bread and some eggs. Would you like me to cook breakfast?"

He lowered his coffee mug slowly, his gaze as warm as the sun on her shoulders, as the ceramic heating her hands. "I didn't bring you out here to wait on me."

"You didn't bring me out here at all. I volunteered to come."

"To help me get ready for the race. Not to serve me."

"It's just breakfast, Trey. And coffee." Even if last night it had been more. Even if the way he was looking at her made her want to climb back into that sleeping bag. "I work much better when my stomach's not growling. I thought it might be the same for you."

"It is, but I'll cook. You made the coffee."

"That's because I can't work at all without caffeine."

"If I'd known that, I would've put on a pot as soon I got up."

"What time *did* you get up?" Judging by the sun's position, she swore it couldn't be any later than seven now. And, yeah, they'd agreed to start working at six.

"Maybe four?" he guessed, giving her a lazy smile.

"But it was almost two…" She let the sentence dangle, finishing the thought privately. She was quite sure he knew exactly what time they'd finally fallen asleep after he'd made love to her.

The question facing her now was where did this relationship—if you could even call it *that*—go from here?

* * * * *

Cardin and Trey are about to find out that
great sex is only the beginning….
Don't miss the fireworks!
Get ready for
A LONG, HARD RIDE
by Alison Kent
Available March 2009,
wherever Blaze books are sold.

CELEBRATE
60 YEARS
OF PURE READING PLEASURE
WITH HARLEQUIN®!

**We'll be spotlighting a different series
every month throughout 2009
to celebrate our 60th anniversary.**

Look for Harlequin® Blaze™ in March!

0-60

*After all, a lot can happen in 60 years,
or 60 minutes...or 60 seconds!*

Find out what's going down in Blaze's
heart-stopping new miniseries *0-60!*
Getting from "Hello" to "How was it?"
can happen fast....

Look for the brand-new **0-60** *miniseries in March 2009!*

www.eHarlequin.com   HBRIDE09

HARLEQUIN® Romance®

This February the Harlequin® Romance series
will feature six Diamond Brides stories featuring
diamond proposals and gorgeous grooms.

Share your dream wedding proposal and you could WIN!

The most romantic entry will win a diamond
necklace and will inspire a proposal in one of
our upcoming Diamond Grooms books in 2010.

In 100 words or less, tell us the most romantic
way that you dream of being proposed to.

For more information, and to enter
the Diamond Brides Proposal contest, please visit
www.DiamondBridesProposal.com

Or mail your entry to us at:

IN THE U.S.: 3010 Walden Ave., P.O. Box 9069, Buffalo, NY 14269-9069
IN CANADA: 225 Duncan Mill Road, Don Mills, ON M3B 3K9

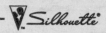

SPECIAL EDITION

Kate's Boys

TRAVIS'S APPEAL

by *USA TODAY* bestselling author

MARIE FERRARELLA

Shana O'Reilly couldn't deny it—family lawyer
Travis Marlowe had some kind of appeal. But
as Travis handled her father's tricky estate
planning, he discovered things weren't what
they seemed in the O'Reilly clan. Would
an explosive secret leave Travis and Shana's
budding relationship in tatters?

Available March 2009
wherever books are sold.

www.eHarlequin.com   SSE65440

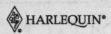

HARLEQUIN®

INTRIGUE

SPECIAL OPS
TEXAS
COWBOY COMMANDO

BY JOANNA WAYNE

When Linney Kingston's best friend dies in
a drowning accident one day after she told
Linney she was leaving her abusive husband,
Linney is convinced the husband killed her. Linney
goes to the one man she knows can help her, an
ex lover who she's never been able to forget—
Navy SEAL Cutter Martin. They will have to
work together to solve the mystery, but can
they leave their past behind them?

Available March 2009 wherever you buy books.

The Inside Romance newsletter has a NEW look for the new year!

Same great content, brand-new look!

The Inside Romance newsletter is a FREE quarterly newsletter highlighting our upcoming series releases and promotions!

Click on the Inside Romance link on the front page of **www.eHarlequin.com** or e-mail us at insideromance@harlequin.ca to sign up to receive your FREE newsletter today!

You can also subscribe by writing to us at: HARLEQUIN BOOKS Attention: Customer Service Department P.O. Box 9057, Buffalo, NY 14269-9057

Please allow 4-6 weeks for delivery of the first issue by mail.

IRNNEW09

REQUEST YOUR FREE BOOKS!

2 FREE NOVELS PLUS 2 FREE GIFTS!

HARLEQUIN®
INTRIGUE®

Breathtaking Romantic Suspense

YES! Please send me 2 FREE Harlequin Intrigue® novels and my 2 FREE gifts (gifts are worth about $10). After receiving them, if I don't wish to receive any more books, I can return the shipping statement marked "cancel." If I don't cancel, I will receive 6 brand-new novels every month and be billed just $4.24 per book in the U.S. or $4.99 per book in Canada, plus 25¢ shipping and handling per book and applicable taxes, if any*. That's a savings of close to 15% off the cover price! I understand that accepting the 2 free books and gifts places me under no obligation to buy anything. I can always return a shipment and cancel at any time. Even if I never buy another book from Harlequin, the two free books and gifts are mine to keep forever.

182 HDN EEZ7   382 HDN EEZK

Name	(PLEASE PRINT)	
Address		Apt. #
City	State/Prov.	Zip/Postal Code

Signature (if under 18, a parent or guardian must sign)

Mail to the Harlequin Reader Service:
IN U.S.A.: P.O. Box 1867, Buffalo, NY 14240-1867
IN CANADA: P.O. Box 609, Fort Erie, Ontario L2A 5X3

Not valid to current subscribers of Harlequin Intrigue books.

Want to try two free books from another line?
Call 1-800-873-8635 or visit www.morefreebooks.com.

* Terms and prices subject to change without notice. N.Y. residents add applicable sales tax. Canadian residents will be charged applicable provincial taxes and GST. Offer not valid in Quebec. This offer is limited to one order per household. All orders subject to approval. Credit or debit balances in a customer's account(s) may be offset by any other outstanding balance owed by or to the customer. Please allow 4 to 6 weeks for delivery. Offer available while quantities last.

Your Privacy: Harlequin is committed to protecting your privacy. Our Privacy Policy is available online at www.eHarlequin.com or upon request from the Reader Service. From time to time we make our lists of customers available to reputable third parties who may have a product or service of interest to you. If you would prefer we not share your name and address, please check here. ☐

H108R

You're invited to join our Tell Harlequin Reader Panel!

By joining our new reader panel you will:

- Receive Harlequin® books—they are FREE and yours to keep with no obligation to purchase anything!
- Participate in fun online surveys
- Exchange opinions and ideas with women just like you
- Have a say in our new book ideas and help us publish the best in women's fiction

In addition, you will have a chance to win great prizes and receive special gifts!
See Web site for details. Some conditions apply.
Space is limited.

To join, visit us at
www.TellHarlequin.com.

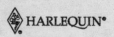
HARLEQUIN®

INTRIGUE®

COMING NEXT MONTH

Available March 10, 2009

#1119 RENEGADE SOLDIER by Pat White
Assignment: The Girl Next Door
NSA Agent Dalton Keen prefers to work alone, until he discovers that his brother is missing. In order to crack the case, he needs the help of civilian Sydney Trent.

#1120 SNOWED IN WITH THE BOSS by Jessica Andersen
Kenner County Crime Unit
A series of suspicious accidents befall millionaire Griffin Vaughn and his secretary, Sophie La Rue, at his newly purchased mountain retreat. Forced to turn to each other for survival, can they figure out who is behind the attacks?

#1121 DESERT ICE DADDY by Dana Marton
Diamonds and Daddies
Sheikh Akeem Abdul would do anything for Taylor Kane, his best friend's little—and off-limits—sister. When the newly divorced Taylor's son is kidnapped, long-denied feelings can no longer be suppressed.

#1122 SECRET DELIVERY by Delores Fossen
Texas Paternity: Boots and Booties
When Alanna Davis disappeared soon after giving birth, Sheriff Jack Whitley stepped in to raise the child he helped deliver. Months later, Alanna has come back for her son, claiming she was kidnapped and held against her will.

#1123 COWBOY COMMANDO by Joanna Wayne
Special Ops Texas
Linney Kingston is on the run with the daughter of her best friend—a friend who she believes was murdered by an abusive husband. The only person to turn to is Cutter Martin, former Navy SEAL and ex-lover.

#1124 MULTIPLES MYSTERY by Alice Sharpe
After giving birth to quadruplets, Olivia Capri needed childhood friend Sheriff Zac Bishop by her side. Can Zac's secret—his feelings for Olivia—keep her and her daughters out of harm's way?

HICNMBPA0209

CLIVE BARKER

"He's an original . . . what he's doing is important and exciting."
—Stephen King

"The first true voice of the next generation of horror writers."
—Ramsey Campbell

"Barker's work possesses a visual flair unusual in any fiction, let alone the horror genre."
—*Books and Bookmen*

"Barker's visions are at one turn horrifyingly stomach-wrenching and at the next flickering with brilliant invention that leaves the reader shaking . . ."
—*Sounds*

"The best new horror writer in years!"
—Michael Moorcock

"Potentially, Barker is a better writer than Stephen King and Peter Straub . . . an immensely talented writer!"
—*Fantasy Review*

"Barker is in a class by himself."
—*Locus*

"A great new talent!"
—James Herbert

"Clive Barker will scare the pants off you."
—*Fangoria*